He just want[...]een.

When they'd be[...] s a pair of old, belo[...]

He dropped his [...] the corner of his eye[...] [...]se, would you finally get over your anger?"

She stabbed her fork into her pie, seeming to focus fiercely on it. "We're not five."

"We were nine." He rubbed the bridge of his nose. "I remember it vividly, since you managed to break it."

"I never intended to break your nose," she muttered.

"I know." He waited a beat. "We survived that. So can't we survive another kiss, even one—I hate to admit—as badly executed as the last one was?" It had been a helluva lot more than a kiss, but he didn't figure she wanted to get into that territory any more than he did.

"It doesn't matter. It was years ago."

He leaned over the arm of his chair toward her. His gaze caught on the wedge of creamy skin showing between the unbuttoned edges of her shirt. Stupid, because there wasn't anything like that between him and Tabby.

Except that one time they were both trying not to think about.

Dear Reader,

For years now, I've received a common question from readers—"What about Tabby?"

Tabby Taggart is one of those backbone characters who has been present in quite a few of the Double C and Weaver-related stories. She's always in my mind, anyway, even if she doesn't make it onto the page. The same can be said of Justin Clay. This young man has been in Tabby's life for as long as she can remember. They've been friends. They've skirted the boundaries of attraction, though frustratingly never quite at the same time. And they've also been at odds.

And all of this has mostly been in my head.

Now I'm delighted that Tabby and Justin have their chance in the sun. And there are (momentarily) slightly fewer voices inside my head!

I hope you enjoy,

Allison

The BFF Bride

—

Allison Leigh

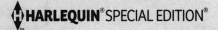

HARLEQUIN® SPECIAL EDITION®

Recycling programs
for this product may
not exist in your area.

ISBN-13: 978-0-373-65968-5

The BFF Bride

Copyright © 2016 by Allison Lee Johnson

Printed in U.S.A.

A frequent name on bestseller lists, **Allison Leigh**'s high point as a writer is hearing from readers that they laughed, cried or lost sleep while reading her books. She credits her family with great patience for the time she's parked at her computer, and for blessing her with the kind of love she wants her readers to share with the characters living in the pages of her books. Contact her at allisonleigh.com.

Visit the Author Profile page at Harlequin.com for more titles.

For my daughters
and the fine young men who love them.

Prologue

Nineteen years ago

"Come on, Tabbers." The boy holding the chains of the swing leaned closer to her and grinned. His weird bluish-purple eyes were full of mischief. And goading.

But that was something Justin Clay had always been good at.

Goading. And a whole lot of it.

Usually, it led to her getting her rear end in trouble with her mom and daddy.

"I told you. I go by *Tabitha* now," she said firmly. She'd just turned nine. Tabitha seemed more fitting than Tabby, much less *Tabbers*.

Justin's eyebrows skyrocketed, and he hooted with laughter, giving the swing's chains a shove so that she shot backward then forward again so unevenly that her bare toes dug into the sand beneath the school's swing set.

"That's bat-crap crazy. You're Tabbers," he said with the annoying superiority he'd developed lately. Catching her chains again, he stopped her forward progress with such a jolt that her chin snapped against her chest. "And you might as well just kiss me. It's gonna happen, one way or another."

She glared at him. "You made me bite my tongue."

If anything, he looked even more devilish. "You going to cry about it?"

She curled her lip. "Not 'cause of you, that's for sure. And I'm *not* gonna kiss you just so you can make Sierra Rasmussen jealous!"

His eyebrows drew together. "You're my best friend," he complained. "We're supposed to help each other out."

Now it was her turn to snort. "Good thing your best friend isn't a boy, then. And I'm still not kissing you!"

"One day you're gonna wanna kiss me," he warned.

Annoyed at the absurdity, she shoved her hand against his chest and pushed him away far enough that she could jump off the swing. Even though his daddy was the tallest person Tabby had ever met, for now, she and Justin were exactly the same height. She looked him straight in the face. "Try it and I'll punch you in the nose," she warned. "I'd sooner kiss a toad than you."

His skinny chest puffed out. "Lotsa toads down at the swimmin' hole, Tabbers."

She puffed out her own chest. It was just as skinny as his. And as flat. Which was fine with her, since boys seemed to have more fun than girls did. At least all the ones she knew around Weaver, anyway. Who wanted to be all prissy and perfect when there were baseball games to play and cow chips to throw and worms to be threaded onto fish hooks? Summer was short enough in Weaver without spending half your time playing indoors with dolls and dress-up. And Justin's granddaddy had the best swimming hole around, out on his Double-C Ranch. She and Justin, along with his cousin Caleb, spent half their summer vacation out there. "I can make you kiss a toad just as easy, Justin Clay, and you know it." She scuffed her bare toes through the sand. The sun was hot as Hades, and now that he'd brought up the topic of swimming, that's all she wanted to do. "I dunno why y'all are so gaga over Sierra, anyway," she groused. The other girl was a year ahead of them in school and the biggest snot around.

"'Cause she's got boobs," he said, as if the answer were obvious. "And Joey Rasmussen says his cousin won't kiss no boy who ain't already kissed someone."

"So? Since when're you interested in kissing girls?"

"Erik's already kissed three girls!"

She rolled her eyes. "Who cares if your brother's kissing girls?"

"I do. So now I gotta kiss someone, and I ain't gonna kiss Caleb!"

She leaned over, pretending to gag. "That's just gross."

"That's just 'cause you don't got any boobs."

She rolled her eyes and shoved his shoulder hard enough to tip him over in the sand.

He laughed, squinting up at her in the sunlight as he stuck out his suntanned hand. "Help me up."

Sighing mightily, she grabbed his hand and yanked.

He sprang easily to his own bare feet and pecked his thin lips against hers before she had a chance to evade him.

Then he danced around her, cackling like a madman, waving his arms over his head in victory. "Told you!"

She made a face. "You are disgusting."

He laughed even harder. "You're just mad 'cause I got my way."

"And *it* was disgusting, too. Still don't know why you gotta keep up with your big brother. I don't gotta keep up with mine."

His smile didn't die, but he stopped his victory dance and dropped his arm over her shoulders, like the best buddies they were. "Come on." He started walking away from the swings. "Let's find Caleb and go out to the swimming hole to catch some toads."

She shrugged. Because she did want to go swimming. "Sure. But first—" She hesitated when they left the sand for the closely shorn green grass covering the rest of the playground.

He hesitated, too, his eyebrows lifting again over his weird bluish-purple eyes. "What?"

She smiled.

Balled her fist.

And punched him in the nose.

Chapter One

"Hey there, Tabby! Happy Thanksgiving." Hope Clay reached for the covered dish in Tabby's gloved hands. "Every year we keep telling you all you need to bring is yourself," she chided with a smile.

"And every year, you know I'm going to bring something to share," Tabby countered easily as she followed the older woman out of the cold November air into the warm, soaring foyer. This year, the rotating Thanksgiving feast was being held at Hope and Tristan Clay's home. The smells of Thanksgiving dinner filled the air, along with the sounds of music and laughter as Tabby pushed the heavy wooden door closed behind her. "I can't take credit for the casserole, though. That's Bubba's doing." Robert "Bubba" Bumble was the cook down at Ruby's Café, which Tabby managed for Hope's two sons, who owned the place.

"How *is* Bubba?" Hope asked over her shoulder as she turned left and sailed into the dining room, where an enormous table was set with white china and sparkling glasses. Next to it—jutting out into the wide hallway—

was a slightly smaller portable table set with disposable plates and cups.

The kids' table, Tabby knew, though the kids generally ranged from her generation down to any child old enough to hold her own spoon. "Bubba's fine," she said wryly. "He's been cooking once a week for Vivian Templeton when her usual chef has the day off."

Hope glanced toward the great room across the wide hallway, as if she were afraid Tabby's words might be overheard. She even put a finger in front of her lips in a silent shush, and her "that's nice" was barely audible.

Tabby had spent as much of her childhood roaming around Hope and Tristan Clay's home as she had around her own. She raised her eyebrows pointedly but lowered her own voice to a whisper while she pulled off her gloves and her coat. "What'd I say?"

"That subject is still a little…sore…with some," Hope replied.

Tabby started to glance toward the great room but managed to stop herself. She'd have to encounter Justin sooner or later. And later was better. "Squire?" she mouthed, more to keep her mind off Hope's youngest son than anything.

Hope nodded, adjusting a few dishes in the middle of the table to make room for Tabby's casserole dish. She looked over her shoulder toward the sound of the crowd in the other room getting all riled up again. "Ever since I married Tristan," she said in a more normal tone, "he's told me how stubborn his father could be. But I've never seen Squire be truly cantankerous until Vivian moved to Weaver. He's downright ornery when it comes to the subject of her." She straightened, her violet eyes studying the table through her stylish glasses.

Tabby knew there was bad blood between Justin's grandfather and Vivian Templeton dating from way back, though. The elderly woman had only arrived in town a little more than a year ago.

"Guess it's good that she's not going to be here for Thanksgiving dinner, then," she said drily. "And I assume there aren't going to be any other Templetons at the table today?"

Hope shook her head, making a face. "That would have been nice, but everyone is still feeling their way after learning they're all related through Tristan's mama."

"Understandable." Tabby's hearing was acutely attuned to the voices coming from the great room, but she kept her gaze strictly on the table. She didn't need to listen too closely to be able to pick Justin's voice out from the others.

He never missed spending Thanksgiving with his parents. He'd never once failed to come home from Boston for the holiday, even if it meant flying in one day and right back out the next—which was what he'd done for the past four years.

"Anything I can do to help get the meal on?" she asked, trying to drown out her memories.

"Bless your heart, honey. You're not on the job here. But I'd be lying if I said I wasn't grateful for your help."

Tabby grinned. "You know me. Always happier being useful and busy than sitting around on my thumbs." And it kept her from having to go into the great room just yet.

She couldn't imagine spending Thanksgiving anywhere else—particularly when her own parents were

away—but being with the Clays on the holiday came
with a price.

Thankfully, her hostess was unaware of Tabby's
thoughts. "You're just like your mama." She tossed
Tabby's coat onto the pile in the study, then drew her
into the kitchen, where nearly every inch of counter
space was covered with one dish or another. "Even
though she and your dad are off visiting your grandma
this year, I'm pleased you still came."

Hope and Jolie Taggart had been best friends for
Tabby's entire life. "You're my second family. Where
else would I be? So put me to work."

Hope gestured at an enormous pot steaming on top
of the stove. "I just need to get the potatoes finished.
Selfishly, I was hoping you'd get here in time to do the
honors. Nobody makes mashed potatoes like you do."

Tabby immediately rolled up the sleeves of her white
blouse and plucked a clean white flour-sack towel out
of a cupboard. "Flattery'll get you everywhere."

Hope laughed. "I'd hoped. I should have everything
you need all set, but if I don't, you know where everything is, anyway."

Smiling, Tabby tied the towel around her waist like
an apron before turning off the flame under the potatoes
and hefting the pot over to the sink to drain it. From the
great room came a loud burst of laughter and hooting
catcalls. "Football game must be a close one." She was
recording it at home to watch later.

"Sounds like." The older woman glanced over her
shoulder when her sister-in-law Jaimie entered carrying
an empty oversize bowl. "More tortilla chips?"

"And salsa." Jaimie smiled at Tabby and bussed her
cheek on her way to the far counter where a variety

of bags were stacked. She deftly tore open a large one and dumped the entire contents into the wooden bowl. "You'd think the hordes hadn't eaten in a week."

"Or that they weren't going to sit down to turkey and ham in only a few minutes." Hope grimaced but handed Jaimie the near-industrial-size container of salsa she pulled from the refrigerator. "I know better than to warn any of them."

Tabby didn't bother hiding her smile as she began scooping the steaming potatoes into the ricer, which Hope had left on the counter next to the sink along with two large crockery bowls. At the diner, she made mashed potatoes by the ton, so the work was simple and easy. But unfortunately, it also allowed her mind to wander down the hallway to the great room and the people there.

Her parents traditionally spent every other Thanksgiving with her grandmother. Tabby's brother, Evan, and his family had gone this year, too. Tabby could have accompanied them. She still wasn't sure why she hadn't.

She grimaced at her own thoughts and scooped more potatoes into the ricer. Steam continued rising up into her face, but she barely noticed as she squeezed out the fluffy fronds, filling the first bowl, then the second.

Who was she kidding?

There were only a few times every year when she was guaranteed to see him. Thanksgiving and Easter. He'd missed Christmas for years. Birthdays? Forget about it.

Seeing him was like picking at a wound that wouldn't heal. She couldn't stop herself, to her own detriment.

She huffed a strand of hair out of her eyes and re-filled the ricer yet again. Fortunately, the contraption was just as large and sturdy as the ones she had at the diner, so the work went quickly.

"Don't you agree?"

She realized the question had been directed at her, and she looked over her shoulder at Hope, only to realize Jaimie had left the kitchen with her chips and salsa and she'd been replaced with another one of her sisters-in-law, Emily. Tabby racked her brains, trying—and failing—to recall their conversation. "Sorry?"

"Thanksgiving is an easier holiday than Christmas," Hope repeated.

"Oh. Sure." It was a lie, and she looked back down at the potatoes. "None of the Christmas gift shopping stress." Just *all* the stress of knowing Justin would be back in town.

She huffed at her hair again and scooped the last of the potatoes into the container, making quick work of them before running the ricer under the faucet.

"Frankly, I don't know what to get *anyone* this year for Christmas," Emily was saying. She moved next to Tabby, holding a saucepan filled with steaming cream and melted butter. "I don't suppose you have any ideas for my son-in-law, do you?"

Tabby made a face and left the ricer to drain while she grabbed a long-handled spoon from the drawer. "*I* don't have any ideas for him, and Evan's my brother." She gestured for Emily to begin pouring the liquid into one of the bowls while she gently stirred the riced potatoes.

Hope stepped up behind Tabby, watching over their shoulders. "I swear, honey, watching you work is like watching a cooking show on television."

At that, Tabby snorted outright. "Only doing the

same thing *your* grandmother taught me to do when I started working at her diner."

"Hope's grandma was quite a cook." Emily drizzled more hot cream into the second bowl at Tabby's prompting. "But I'm just thankful Ruby taught you how to make her cinnamon rolls."

"My hips aren't that happy," Hope said drily. "I can't tell you how many times Gram tried to teach me how to make her rolls." She shook her head. "I can make them, but not like she could. Or you." She patted Tabby's shoulder. "She would roll over in her grave hearing me say so, but I think yours have got hers beat."

"Good grief, don't say that." Tabby looked up at the ceiling, as though she was waiting for lightning to strike. "I loved Ruby Leoni, too, but oh, man, did she have a temper."

Hope laughed. "You nearly finished there, honey?"

Tabby focused on her work again, giving the creamy potatoes a final stir. "All set." She picked up both bowls, cradling them against her hips. "You want them on the table now?"

"That was twenty pounds of Yukon Golds. I should get one of the boys—"

"No worries. I've got them." Tabby quickly cut her off and carried the bowls out to the dining room, placing one at one end of the main table and the other on the kids' table. Hope and Emily followed along, bearing platters of freshly carved roast turkey and glazed ham.

"I have a good mind to let them all watch football while we feast on our own," Hope said when a caterwaul of cheers and jeers burst out from the other room. She adjusted one of the platters just so and stood back to admire the display.

Emily, meanwhile, was counting off chairs and place settings. "I think we're a few short," she warned.

"We're always a few short," Hope returned. "That's what happens these days when nearly the whole family turns out." She stepped to the archway opening onto the wide hallway. "Food's on," she called briskly. Her one-time schoolteacher's voice cut across the racket of televised sports and thirtysome family members debating the latest call. Considering they weren't all rooting for the same team, it was chaotic, to say the least.

Nevertheless, at Hope's announcement, the television volume immediately went mute and those thirtysome individuals turned en masse toward the dining room.

She didn't rush.

For as long as she could remember, she'd sat at the kids' table.

"Tabby! I didn't even hear you come in." Hope's husband, Tristan, grabbed her up in a bear hug that lifted her right off her toes. "Thank God we'll have decent mashed potatoes." He kissed her forehead and dropped her back down. "When Tag said he and your ma were visiting Helen this year, I was afraid it was gonna be boxed potatoes."

Hope gave him a pinch. "Since when have I *ever* made you mashed potatoes from a box?"

The tall man, still blond in his sixties, grinned and gave Tabby a quick wink before he made his way toward the head of the big table, jostling his relations while Hope directed butts to seats and ultimately determined that Emily had been right. They were short of chairs. Erik—Hope and Tristan's eldest—immediately pigeonholed his adopted son, Murphy, to help him search down more.

Tabby, long used to the process, just moved out of

the way as far as possible and bit back a chuckle when Squire brushed past everyone to take the first seat— which happened to be Tristan's at the head of the table. "All that fancy money you earn, boy, seems you ought to have a bigger table 'n' chairs."

"That's my chair, old man," Tristan said mildly. But Tabby could see by the humor in his blue eyes that he wasn't offended. Or surprised. "And the way this family keeps growing, we'd need a reception hall to seat everyone at one table."

Erik and Murphy returned with two more chairs and a piano bench, and the shuffling began again.

"Same thing happens every year."

Tabby stiffened inwardly at the deep voice. She didn't look at the tall man who'd stopped next to her, bumping his elbow companionably against hers. She didn't need to.

There'd been a time when she knew everything there was to know about Justin Clay. And he'd known everything about her. They'd been best friends.

Now...they weren't.

"Yes, it does. Some people like that," she answered smoothly and moved toward the kids' table. She sat down in the only spare seat, next to fourteen-year-old Murphy, who was eyeing her from the corner of his eye the way he had been for at least a year now. On her other side was April Reed—one of Squire's grandchildren courtesy of his long-ago marriage to Gloria Day.

"Haven't seen you since last summer." She greeted April with a smile, all the while painfully aware of Justin trading barbs with Caleb Buchanan behind her. "You cut your hair. I like it."

The young woman flushed and looked pleased that

Tabby had noticed. She toyed with the shoulder-length auburn bob. "Job hunting," she said. "Thought it looked more in keeping with a suit."

"Looks great." Tabby tugged the ends of her own hair. It was riddled with wayward waves. "I've been thinking of cutting mine, too."

"Why?" Justin nudged Murphy's shoulder. "Scoot your chair over, kid."

Murphy made a face, but he moved over enough to accommodate Justin, who pushed a backless stool into the space and straddled it. "Your hair's been like that as long as I can remember."

Tabby knew he wasn't trying to get cozy with her. There was simply a finite amount of space available for chairs and bodies. She looked away from the jeans-clad thigh nudging against her. "All the more reason it's time for a change, then, right, April?"

"I suppose. But I've always thought you had gorgeous hair. Such a dark brown and so glossy."

Tabby couldn't help but laugh a little at that. "Grass is always greener, my friend with the smooth red hair." She leaned over the table a little, mostly so she could shift away from that damned masculine thigh. "So, how *is* the job hunt going out in Arizona? It's advertising, right?"

"Dad wants me to work for him at Huffington," she said, referring to the network of sports clinics he operated around the United States. "The Phoenix location is getting huge. But I want to make my mark on my own."

"Makes sense."

Justin jostled Tabby's arm. "Remember when you wanted to go to Europe to make your mark on the great art world?"

"Lofty dreams of a teenaged girl," she said dismissively. She wasn't going to let him bait her. "*I* learned I was perfectly happy right here in Weaver," she told April, though the words were aimed at Justin. "This is my home. I can't imagine living anywhere else."

"Ruby's would have to shut right down," someone interjected from the other table. "Weaver would never be the same."

Tabby rolled her eyes. "Erik and Justin own the place." She still didn't look at the man beside her. "They'd hire someone else to manage it."

"There's a nasty thought," Erik said. He was sitting at the main table next to his wife, Isabella, and didn't look unduly concerned.

The same couldn't be said of their son. "You're *not* gonna leave, are you?" Murphy gave her a horrified look.

She lifted her hands peaceably. "I'm not going anywhere!"

Justin jostled her again. "Do you even still paint?"

If she'd have been five—or maybe even twenty-five—she would have just elbowed him right back. Preferably in the ribs, hard enough to leave a mark. Because the Justin she'd grown up with could take as well as he could give. "Yes, I still paint." Her voice was even.

"Absolutely, she still paints!" Sydney, who was married to Derek—yet another one of Justin's plentiful cousins—called from the far end of the other table. Their toddler son was sitting in a high chair between them. "An old friend of mine who owns a gallery in New York has sold a couple dozen of her pieces! He wants her to give up working at Ruby's and focus only on painting."

Tabby shifted, uncomfortable with the weight of everyone's eyes turning toward her. "I'm not quitting Ruby's," she assured them, wondering how on earth the conversation had gotten so off track.

"We know that, Tab," Erik assured her calmly. Of the two brothers, he was the active partner in the diner, though he pretty much left the day-to-day stuff to her.

Squire cleared his throat loudly. Tabby was quite sure if he'd had his walking stick handy, he'd have thumped it on the floor for emphasis the way he tended to do. "We gonna sit here and jabber all the livelong day, or get to eating?"

Tristan chuckled. "Eat."

"Not before we say grace," Gloria said mildly. And inflexibly. So they all bowed their heads while Gloria said the blessing.

Justin leaned close to her again. "Nothing changes," he murmured almost soundlessly.

Tabby's jaw tightened. She looked from her clasped hands to the insanely handsome, violet-eyed man sitting only inches away from her.

"You changed," she whispered back.

Then she looked back at her hands and closed her eyes. Gloria was still saying grace.

Tabby just prayed that Justin would go away again, and the sooner the better.

He'd been her best friend.

But he was still her worst heartbreak.

Chapter Two

His mother might have put the meal on the table, but it was up to her husband and sons to cart everything back to the kitchen when the meal was done.

Not even the Thanksgiving holiday—or televised football games—got them out of that particular task.

So even though Justin generally would rather poke sharp sticks into his eyes than load a dishwasher, he did his fair share, carting stacks of plates and glasses from the dining room to the kitchen, following on Erik's heels.

And while the rest of the women in the family had pitched in to help Hope, the three men were brutally left on their own by their fellows.

"Typical," Justin muttered, dumping the plates on the counter next to the sink his dad was filling with soap and water. "Couldn't even get Caleb to help."

Erik chuckled. He was five years older than Justin and he good-naturedly threw a clean dish towel at him. "You ever help clean up when we have a meal at his folks' place?" The question was rhetorical. "Be glad that half the crowd today used disposable plates."

Justin had personally filled a big bag with the trash.

He would have been happy to fill a half dozen of them if it meant not having to load a dishwasher.

"Stop grousing and get it done," their father ordered. "Dessert's waiting on us, and Squire never likes waiting for his dessert."

"The old man looks good," Justin said. He left the dish towel on the counter and pulled open the dishwasher. He began to load it methodically, mechanically transferring the items his dad rinsed into the racks.

"He's gonna run for city council," Tristan said, shaking his head as if he still couldn't believe it. "There's a special election coming up in February."

"Squire?" Justin couldn't help but laugh at the notion of his ninetysome-year-old grandfather sitting at a council meeting. "That ought to shake things up around Weaver. He's always hated politicians."

"Which is the reason why he figures an old rancher ought to try his hand at it." Erik started filling containers with the leftover food. They heard a cheer from the great room and he groaned a little.

"Shouldn't have bet against Casey on the game," Justin said knowingly. Their cousin had an uncanny gift for picking winners. "What're you gonna lose to him this time?"

"Week out at the fishing cabin. And I haven't lost yet."

"When's the last time you won a bet against him?" Tristan stacked more rinsed plates on the counter. "What's going on with that promotion of yours, Jus?"

Justin added the dishes to the rack with a little more force than necessary. "Not a damn thing."

"You crack those plates, son, you'll be the one to face up to your mother."

Justin straightened again and met his father's gaze. "It's gotten…complicated."

Erik blew out a soft whistle. "Probably happens when you're dating the boss's daughter. Warned you."

"I didn't get the job at CNJ Pharmaceuticals nine years ago because of Gillian. I won't lose it because of her, either." He was trusting that his relationship with Charles Jennings, her father and the owner of the company, was on firmer ground than that, at least. He swiped his damp hands down his jeans and retrieved a cold bottle of beer from the refrigerator. "And we stopped seeing each other almost half a year ago."

"Thank God," Erik muttered. "Woman was a nose-bleed."

Justin grimaced. "I don't sneer at your choice of women."

Erik grinned. "How could you? Izzy is the perfect girl."

Justin couldn't deny the truth of that, though he liked arguing with his brother merely for the sake of it. And he didn't really want to think about Gillian, anyway. Because she *was* a nosebleed, even though his brother shouldn't rub it in. And even though it had taken Justin several long years to face it.

He toyed with the beer cap but didn't actually twist it open. "The complication isn't because of Charles's daughter. He's put me on a special project we've had some problems with. If I can bring it in on time, the VP position should be mine." Making him the youngest vice president in the company's century-long history.

"Give me cows over pharmaceuticals," Erik said, hanging his arm over Justin's shoulder. "But I suppose if anyone can do it, it's my genius little brother, Dr. Justin Clay."

Justin shrugged off the arm. He had a PhD in microbiology and immunology, and dual master's degrees in computer science and chemistry. But he rarely used the title that went with the PhD. The fact was, he'd often felt a little out of step among his extended ranching family, even though his computer-geek father had bucked that trend, too.

"I want to work on the project from Weaver," he announced, and saw the look his brother and dad exchanged. "I'll be able to concentrate on it better here. I figure Aunt Bec might clear the way for me to work at the hospital, since she runs the place."

"Rebecca probably can, though that's—"

"Rebecca probably can what?" Justin's eldest uncle, Sawyer, entered the kitchen carrying several empty beer bottles.

"Approve space in the new lab they're building for a project I'm working on for CNJ. The company will cover all the costs, of course."

"Sell that to my wife," Sawyer advised wryly. "Every day for the past two years I've been hearing about problems with that lab she's trying to get built. Construction delays. Cost overruns. Losing the lab director didn't help, and now it's that fund-raiser event they're having in a few weeks." He dumped the bottles in the recycling basket and pulled open the refrigerator to retrieve several more beers. "You gonna be done in here soon? The old man's getting impatient for dessert. He's been debating pumpkin pie versus pecan versus chocolate cream for the past half hour."

"We'd be done sooner if we had some help," Tristan told his brother in a pointed tone.

Sawyer just laughed, snatched the unopened bottle out of Justin's hands to add to his collection and left the kitchen again.

When Justin went to the refrigerator, he found the shelf empty of beer.

"Snooze you lose, son," Tristan said. "Just because you choose to live in Boston doesn't mean you're excluded from that basic fact." He pointed a thumb at the stack of rinsed dishes still waiting to be loaded.

Sawyer's intrusion was followed almost immediately by the rest of his brothers—first Jefferson, ostensibly to make sure there was still hot coffee on the stove, then Matthew and Daniel together, who made no bones that they were wanting their dessert, too.

"Nothing changes," Justin repeated when the kitchen eventually cleared.

"Ever consider that there are times that's a comfort?" Tristan finally turned off the faucet and dried his hands on a towel.

"Never thought so before, particularly."

His father's gaze wasn't unsympathetic. But then, back in his day, Tristan had left Weaver for a good long while, too. Until he'd married Hope Leoni and they'd settled in Weaver permanently. He'd established a little company called Cee-Vid that became a huge player in consumer electronics, and Hope had taught at the elementary school and then ended up the head of the school board.

"Someday—" Tristan's voice was unusually reflective "—you might sit up and realize one of the most disturbing things in life is finding out that something you'd counted on never changing has already done so, without you ever having noticed." Then he tossed the towel on the counter and left the kitchen, too.

Frowning, Justin turned toward Erik. "What's with him?"

"Nothing that's new. You're just not usually around to see it."

"What's *that* supposed to mean?"

"Just a fact," Erik said mildly. "You're in Boston. You don't see the day-to-day effects of the crap he deals with. And I'm not talking about Cee-Vid."

No. Erik was talking about the real work their father did. The secretive, frequently dangerous world of Hollins-Winword's black operations, where their father was second in command. Cee-Vid was the legitimate front that hid the covert work, which Justin and Erik knew about but rarely discussed.

"It's been a hard year," Erik said.

"Isn't it always hard?"

"Harder than most," his brother amended. "I think he's getting tired of it."

"Then he should quit."

"Who should quit what?" Izzy entered the kitchen, her brownish-black gaze bouncing from her husband's face to Justin's and back again.

Erik just looped his hands around her waist and tugged her close. "Are you hungry again?"

She smiled impishly. "For pecan pie. I came to help with the dishes in order to get at dessert more quickly."

"Too late." Justin stuffed the last glass in the dishwasher and closed the door. He'd arrived barely an hour before they'd sat down for dinner, so he hadn't had an opportunity to catch up very much with anyone, including his sister-in-law. "You're looking better than ever, Iz."

She turned in the circle of his brother's arms and beamed at him.

It took a few seconds for Justin to notice the way their linked hands were clasped over her belly. But when he did, it took less than a second for him to realize why. "Holy—" He broke off. "You're pregnant?"

Izzy glanced up into Erik's eyes. "Looks like we're announcing it today whether we planned to or not."

Erik smiled slowly and Justin felt an unfamiliar—and unwanted—jolt of envy. His brother looked so damn happy. So content. And Justin felt so…not.

Still, his brother *was* happy. And Justin was genuinely glad for that. And Isabella…well, she'd always been a looker with her white-blond hair and dark eyes. And now she had an extra shine around her.

He blew out a breath because his throat actually felt tight. "Damn. Congratulations." He wrapped them both in a big hug, which made Izzy laugh and complain, because she was a good foot shorter and couldn't breathe while stuck between two big men. When Justin finally stepped back, envious or not, he knew he had a big, stupid grin on his face. Probably one that matched Erik's. "So when's he—"

"She," Erik corrected.

"Due?"

"The *baby*," Isabella said with a soft laugh, "is due the end of April. We're not going to find out early what we're having."

"Murphy knows there's a baby, though?"

Isabella nodded. "We told him yesterday."

"He figures it's his right to make the announcement today," Erik said wryly. "Being the big brother and all."

"Sounds like he's got the Clay tendencies down, born into them or not." He leaned over and kissed Isabella's cheek. "You're going to be a great mom, all over again." The circumstances leading to her becoming Murphy's mom had been tragic. But they'd ultimately prompted their move to Weaver, where they'd found Erik and become a family.

She blinked, looking teary through her smile. "Thanks." She sniffed quickly. "We'll all learn together, anyway."

"So…pretty much status quo," Erik said wryly.

Isabella chuckled and swiped her cheek. "Pretty much." They all looked back at the sound of footsteps as Tabby entered the kitchen.

The easy smile on Tabby's face faded a bit as she hesitated. She didn't look at Justin. "Um… I just came to help get the pies—"

Isabella quickly moved out of Erik's arms. "Squire's probably getting testy," she said with a knowing laugh. She picked up two of the pies sitting on one counter and handed them to Erik before she grabbed two more. "Bring the plates," she said as she and Erik left the kitchen.

Tabby quickly snatched up a stack of pie plates and started to follow, but Justin grabbed her arm. "Wait a sec."

"They can't eat pie without plates."

"My family? You're kidding, right? They could eat without hands. You've been giving me the cold shoulder since I got here. Don't you think it's time we got past that?"

Her brown eyes—usually warm and shiny as melted chocolate—were unreadable. "I don't know what you're talking about."

"Your lying's on par with your French. You remember French, right? I had to help you pass it in high school."

Her lips tightened. She pulled free and opened a drawer to extract a cake server. "If you want a slice of Gloria's chocolate cream, you'd better get out there quick."

He was tired of the chasm that had developed between them, even though he knew he was the cause of it in the first place. "Come on, Tabbers. We were friends long before—"

She lifted her eyebrows and gave him a look that stopped any further discussion. "Pie's a big deal in this house at Thanksgiving. Or have you forgotten that, living the fancy life in Boston?"

She turned on her heel, and her glossy hair flipped around her shoulders as she left the kitchen.

He exhaled, pinching the bridge of his nose.

There were a few things he'd always counted on. The love and support of his big, crazy family. His own ability to figure out a convoluted puzzle. And the easygoing friendship of one Tabitha Taggart.

Yeah, he knew he'd messed up with her pretty good, but that had been four years ago. Stacked up against the rest of their lifelong friendship, couldn't one monumentally stupid move on his part be forgotten?

Or at least forgiven?

He blew out another breath and grabbed the last two pies that were sitting on the counter and carried them out to the dining room.

"Oh, good. Set them there, honey." His mom pointed with the long knife she was using to cut the pies, and he set them on the table. She'd already divvied out two pumpkin pies onto plates. "There's a gallon of home-made vanilla ice cream in the freezer. Would you mind getting that, too? Oh, and the glass bowl in the fridge with the whipped cream."

He turned around and retrieved the items. When he got back to the dining room, she'd finished plating the chocolate cream. He grabbed a slice while the grabbing was good and went back into the living room. It was a huge space. Always had been, with three couches long enough that even his dad—nearly six and a half feet tall—could stretch out, and an eclectic collection of side chairs and recliners. With all the family around—or close to it, anyway—there still weren't enough seats. So folding chairs had been dragged in. And cushions to lean against on the floor.

He took the same corner he'd been in before dinner. Since he'd forgotten a fork, he picked up the wedge of pie in his fingers and took a bite.

"Neanderthal." His cousin JD dropped a plastic fork onto his plate as she carried two plates to the couch closest to him. She handed one to her husband, Jake, then sat down on the floor in front of him, her legs stretched out. Justin knew she'd have sat on Jake's knee if it hadn't already been occupied by their sleeping little boy, Tucker.

Justin jerked his chin toward her. "When does Tuck start kindergarten?"

"Next fall." She looked over her shoulder at the little boy and gently swiped his messy brown hair off his forehead. "He was upset that he didn't get to go this year."

"Gonna have any more?"

She and Jake shared a look.

"Yes," she said.

"No," he said.

Justin hid his smile around a bite of his grandma's delicious pie. Tucker had been born very prematurely. Though it looked like JD had gotten over it and was ready to go again, her husband had not.

"When're you gonna get yourself a wife?" Squire's voice carried across the room, and there was no question he'd directed his words to Justin. The old man was looking straight at him.

For some reason, Justin found himself glancing toward Tabby across the room.

"Justin's never gonna get married," Axel—yet another cousin—drawled before he could answer. "He told us all that when he graduated from high school. He was gonna go off and cure disease and save the world. Remember?"

Justin grimaced.

"He'd just had his heart broken by—what was her name?" His dad's eyes narrowed as he thought back. "Pretty girl. Short blond hair."

"Colleen," his mother called out from the dining room.

"Collette," Tabby corrected. "Summers. Her dad worked for the electric company."

"Collette Summers," Caleb repeated. "She was so hot."

"What do you know about hot? You were dating Kelly Rasmussen," Justin reminded.

"Whatever happened to Kelly," someone asked.

"Can I tell 'em *now*?"

Everyone looked toward Murphy, who'd loudly interrupted the conversation.

Erik grinned. "Go for it, Murph."

The boy uncoiled from his seat on the floor, standing up to his full height. "We're getting a baby," he announced, his cheeks red, his eyes beaming.

Isabella laughed and reached out to squeeze his hand. "I don't know about *getting*," she said humorously. "But we're definitely having one. Should be making his or her arrival sometime next April."

Justin's mother had finally finished cutting pies. She stared at them slack jawed for a moment before virtually vaulting over people and furniture to grab Izzy in a hug. "Another grandbaby." She looped her other arm around Murphy and kissed his forehead. "A grandson has been wonderful, and this baby is going to be fabulous!"

Hope had about a half second before the rest of the crew started climbing around them to give their own hugs.

When Justin got the third elbow in the head during the process, he gave up his corner spot and found refuge across the room in one of the vacated chairs.

Which happened to be next to Tabby's spot on the floor. "If you get up and move now, someone's gonna notice," he told her under his breath.

Her lips tightened, but she stayed where she was, recrossing her denim-covered legs again just as she'd done when they were little kids. Only difference now was that the legs those jeans covered were long and shapely, instead of skinny with scrapes all over 'em.

At least, he was assuming they weren't all scraped

up anymore. He hoped not, anyway. Because her skin was smooth and creamy—

He pinched the bridge of his nose, cutting off the memory. It was as unwanted as the envy he'd felt at his own brother's happiness.

He just wanted things the way they used to be.

Easy. Comfortable and familiar as a pair of old, beloved boots.

He dropped his hand and looked at her from the corner of his eyes. "If I let you punch me in the nose, would you finally get over your mad?"

She stabbed her fork into her pie, seeming to focus fiercely on it. "We're not five."

"We were nine." He rubbed the bridge of his nose. "I remember it vividly, since you managed to break it."

She huffed out a breath. "I never intended to break your nose," she muttered.

"I know." He waited a beat. "We survived that. So can't we survive another kiss, even one—I hate to admit—as badly executed as it was?" It had been a helluva lot more than a kiss, but he didn't figure she wanted to get into that territory any more than he did.

He was right. "It doesn't matter. It was years ago."

He leaned over the arm of his chair toward her. His gaze caught on the wedge of creamy skin showing between the unbuttoned edges of her shirt. And he couldn't look away. Which was stupid, because there wasn't anything like that between him and Tabby.

Except that one time they were both trying not to think about.

"And things haven't been right between us since," he said.

She slowly sucked a smear of chocolate from her

thumb, taking long enough for him to get his eyes off her chest and onto her lips.

Now he was focused on her soft pink lips pursed around her thumb. How freaking stupid was that.

She finally lowered her hand, wiping it on her crumpled paper napkin. Then she rose to her feet with as much agility as she'd had when they were nine. "You're gonna leave again before any of us can blink, so why does it even matter?"

Slipping his empty plate out of his fingers, she worked her way around the horde of people blocking the way and left the room.

Chapter Three

"Stupid. Stupid, stupid, *freaking* stupid." Tabby was still kicking herself an hour later when she got home to the triplex she'd bought the previous year.

If she'd wanted to prove that she wasn't affected by Justin Clay, she'd failed.

Monumentally.

Running out the way she had while everyone was still congratulating Izzy and Erik over the baby?

"Stupid," she muttered for the fiftieth time while she made her way through the apartment, flipping on lights as she went until she reached her bedroom at the back.

She tugged the tails of her white shirt free from her jeans and yanked it over her head, not bothering with the buttons. Her bra—a glorified name for the hank of lace and elastic that was all her meager bust had ever required—followed. She'd ditched her cowboy boots at the front door already; now she kicked off her jeans, pitching all of the clothing in the general direction of her closet before pulling a football jersey over her head.

"Stupid," she said again. Just for good measure and because she evidently liked punishing herself.

In stocking feet, she went back to the living room and flipped on the television to watch the football game she'd recorded.

"He'll be gone tomorrow," she said to herself. "You won't have to think about him for another six months." The sounds of the football game followed her into her kitchen, but it didn't drown out the cackle of laughter inside her head.

Since when had Justin's absence ever stopped her from thinking about him?

She shoved a glass under the refrigerator's ice dispenser, but not even that racket outdid the cackle.

Which just annoyed her all the more.

She thought she'd prepared herself for seeing him.

Every year, she thought she'd prepared herself for seeing him.

And every year, she failed.

The phone hanging on the wall next to the fridge suddenly rang, and she snatched up the receiver. "What?"

A brief hesitation, then female laughter greeted her. "Criminy, Tab. Happy Thanksgiving to you, too."

Tabby forced her shoulders to relax. "Sam," she greeted. "Aren't you still on duty?" Samantha Dawson was the only female officer with the local sheriff's department.

"Taking my supper break."

"Too bad you have to work on a holiday."

"Not for my bank account. Double-time pay. How was the big get-together over at the Clays'?"

Even though Tabby had gotten pretty friendly with Sam over the past few years, the other woman wasn't privy to the history between Tabby and Justin.

Nobody was.

"It was fine." She shook herself. "A lot of fun. Always is. Have you heard how Hayley's day went?"

Hayley Banyon was a good friend of Sam's. She was also a Templeton, and as such, would have had as much reason or more to be at the Clay family fete as Tabby, since she was one of the relations the Clays had recently learned about.

"I saw her, actually," Sam said. "Needed her professional help on a family dispute call that came in. She said she was grateful for the call, if that gives you any hint."

It did. "That's too bad." If there was dissension between Vivian Templeton and Squire, according to Hayley there was even more between Vivian and her own sons. One of whom was Hayley's father. "So did you call to shoot the breeze, or what's up?"

"Just checking whether you're opening the diner tomorrow."

"Yup." She'd be there before 4:00 a.m. as usual to get the cinnamon rolls going. "Pool tournament at Colbys kicks off tomorrow and I'm figuring I'll get overflow business from it like I did last year. Why?"

"Promised a dozen to Dave Ruiz if he covers a shift for me next week."

"They'll be hot and fresh by six, same as always."

"Good enough. See you then."

Tabby was still smiling when she hung up. The phone rang again before she had a chance to take her hand off the receiver, and she picked it up again. "Let me guess," she said on a laugh. "Two dozen?"

"Two dozen what?"

Her nerves tightened right back up at the sound of

Justin's voice. "I thought you were somebody else. What do you want?"

"I want you to get over the damn stick you got up your—"

She hung up on him.

It took only a second before the phone rang again.

She disconnected the phone line, and it went silent.

Then she turned back to the refrigerator and poured cold tea over the ice in her glass, flicked off the light in the kitchen and went back to the living room to watch her recorded football game.

She fell asleep on the couch before halftime and woke up around 3:00 a.m. to the fuzzy, bluish-white light from the blank television screen.

There was no point in going to bed when she needed to be at the diner soon, anyway.

Rubbing the sleep from her face, she went to shower and got dressed for the day.

Thirty minutes later, with her damp hair hidden beneath a bright blue knit cap and her gloved hands shoved deep in the pockets of her wool coat, she walked the three blocks from her triplex to the restaurant and let herself in the rear door. She didn't need to turn on any lights to make her way through the back of the diner, because aside from updating an appliance here and there over the years, nothing significant had changed since she'd started working there as a teenager.

She went out to the front of the restaurant, where the glass windows overlooked Main Street, and started fresh coffee brewing. With that delicious aroma following her, she went back into the kitchen, turned on the lights and got down to work.

By the time she heard the back door open again,

she had three baking sheets of cinnamon rolls cooling on the racks and was sliding two more into the oven. "Grab that third sheet from the counter, would you?"

She looked over her shoulder, expecting Bubba.

But it was Justin who picked up the large metal pan. "This one?"

Her lips tightened, and she took the sheet pan from him, sliding it into the oven along with the others and closing the door. "Come to check on your investment?"

She didn't wait for an answer and went back out through the swinging door to the front, where she poured herself a cup of coffee. It wasn't quite 6:00 a.m. yet, but she unlocked the door and flipped the Closed sign to Open, anyway.

When she turned back, Justin was sitting on one of the red vinyl–upholstered stools at the counter. He was wearing dark gray running pants and a zippered jacket with *CNJ* printed on the stand-up collar.

His clothes looked expensive. And darn it all, they fit his tall, exceptional physique as if they'd been tailored for him. Which, for all she knew, they had been. He'd admitted quite a few years ago that he not only had his suits tailored, but his shirts, as well. His precious Gillian had seen to that.

Since Tabby didn't want to think about that, she focused on everything above his neck. His thick, short hair was damp, making the blond strands look brown. He'd obviously showered. Her nose was even prickling from the vaguely spicy scent of his soap. Or…whatever.

"You need a shave." She flipped over a thick white mug, filled it with coffee and pushed it in front of him.

His long fingers circled the mug. "You should keep the door locked when you're here by yourself."

"Please. Be mighty hard for customers to come in to Ruby's if I kept the doors locked whenever I happen to be alone." Hard for customers. Hard for intruders.

She pushed aside the thought and went back through the swinging door, pulled on clean plastic gloves and turned out the first batch of rolls, deftly packing several up individually, then punched down the dough that was rising in an enormous steel bowl.

He hadn't budged when she went back out to the front.

She deposited the pastry boxes next to the register, threw away the gloves, refilled her coffee and leaned back against the rear counter, studying him over the brim of her cup. His eyes were bloodshot. Which, annoyingly, just seemed to make the violet color stand out that much more. "Tie one on last night?"

His jaw canted to one side. He shook his head and squinted as he sipped the steaming-hot coffee. "Should have. Couldn't sleep, anyway. At least then it would've been worthwhile."

She smiled sweetly. "I slept like a baby." On the couch. Plagued by dreams about him, only to wake with a crick in her neck that still made it hurt to turn her head too far to the left.

"Were you always this much of a witch, Tab?"

Despite everything, she felt a stab of some unidentified emotion. "Isn't that how spinsters are supposed to act?"

He leaned on his elbows and looked at her through his lashes. "Twenty-eight is spinsterhood now?"

She sipped her coffee. It was to some old-fashioned folks around Weaver. But truthfully?

She felt that stab again. Regret, perhaps. Maybe loss.

It was hard to tell. When it came to Justin, things had started getting complicated long before they'd become adults. "Close enough to be a regular at Dee Crowder's spinster poker night."

"'Spinster' sounds like you're seventy-five and still pining for your first kiss." He gave her that through-the-lashes look again. "And I know you don't qualify there. Hell." His lips twitched suddenly. "I remember when Caleb kissed you when we were freshmen in high school."

About the time when she'd wished Justin would have been interested in kissing her. But he'd never been interesting in kissing her for *her*. She'd always been a substitute on that score. A substitute he'd left behind the same way he'd left behind Weaver.

"Doesn't count," she said promptly. "It was a practice kiss. He was afraid he'd mess up when he planted his first one on Kelly Rasmussen."

Justin's head came up, his expression genuinely surprised. "I always figured you gave him the same response you gave me when we were nine. Without the broken nose."

It was nearly six. She figured Sloan McCray, one of the deputy sheriffs, would be showing his face soon before he went on duty. And frankly, she would be grateful for the interruption.

She flipped on the radio and glanced over the stack of to-go cups she kept near the big brewer. "If he'd done it without permission in order to make Kelly jealous, I probably would have given him the same response." She lifted her shoulder. "Apples and oranges, though."

"I didn't kiss you to make Sierra jealous."

"And you didn't sleep with me four years ago to

make—what's her name? Oh, right. Gillian." The name was seared on her brain. "That wasn't an attempt to get her to sit up and take notice of you?"

"How many times do you want me to apologize for that?"

"I don't know. Maybe a few million." She looked past him when the front door opened, making the little bell on top jingle softly. "Good morning, Deputy. Get you the usual?"

"Yeah. Thanks, Tabby." Sloan stepped up to the counter and handed her his insulated travel mug for the coffee. She turned and filled it while he greeted Justin. "How's life in Boston?"

"Cold," Justin admitted. "Not as cold as here—" he glanced at Tabby "—but still cold. How's your wife?"

"Keeping me warm," Sloan drawled. "Very warm."

"And the boy—Dillon, right?"

"Growing like a weed," Tabby said, turning to hand the deputy his coffee mug, along with one of the pastry boxes. "He and Abby came by last week. Dillon's going to be a heartbreaker one of these days."

"Fortunately, I think we've got a few years yet before we have to worry about that." He pulled out his wallet.

She waggled her finger at him. "You know your money is no good here, Deputy."

"And you know I'm gonna argue."

"Justin's half owner of this place. Tell him, Justin."

"What Tabby said," Justin said obediently, without moving a muscle. "Easier to go along with her than argue, because you'll never win. Trust me."

Sloan stuffed a few dollars in the empty tip jar by the register. "You won't give that back, because I know it gets split among your crew." He took a sip from his mug, turning his gaze to Justin again. "You in town for the long weekend? Going to play in Colbys' pool tournament?"

Tabby busied herself restacking the pastry boxes. Justin would be gone by nightfall just like always. He never stayed the entire Thanksgiving weekend. At least on that score, she could relax a little.

"I'm here until January. But no, I leave the pool games to my brother."

She accidentally dropped the boxes and they scattered. "January!"

As Sloan leaned over and picked up the boxes that had landed on the floor, the radio attached to his belt crackled. He adjusted the sound and set the boxes on the counter. "Sure I'll be seeing more of you then," he said. He gestured with his mug and picked up his own pastry box. "Thanks, Tabby."

"You bet." She waited until the deputy departed before she focused on Justin again. *"January?"*

"I know the thought's horrifying to you, but try to dial it down a little." He came around the counter and refilled his coffee mug.

And even though she wanted to tell him to get back on his own side of the counter, she couldn't very well do so.

Like it or not, he *was* her boss. It didn't matter that he'd always left the decision making to his brother when it came to Ruby's. But Justin was still half owner. It wasn't something she dwelled on, but when they were standing right there in Ruby's, it was kind of hard to forget.

She mentally counted to ten and tried again. "You're here until January?" Calmer or not, her voice had still gone a little hoarse at the end. But she held up her chin as if it hadn't. "Why is that?"

"I'll be working on a project here for CNJ. At the hospital, mostly. My aunt cleared it last night, though she's going to have me jumping through a few more hoops than I expected because of it."

Tabby let his answer roll around in her head a few times. "Why can't you work on it in Boston at that big state-of-the-art laboratory you love?"

"Too many distractions there."

"Gillian being one of them?"

"Yes, but not the way you th—" He went silent when the bell over the door jingled again, and Sam strolled in.

She hadn't yet changed from her jogging gear into her uniform. Tabby waited for the usual male reaction to register in Justin's expression as he took in the sight of Sam's figure lovingly outlined from neck to ankle in vibrant, clinging purple fabric.

But he didn't do the typical double take like all the other guys.

Instead, he nodded politely at Sam and turned back to stare into his coffee mug while Tabby rang up a dozen rolls.

If he was so crazy about Gillian that a beautiful woman like Samantha didn't even merit a glance, what was he doing making Tabby's life harder by sticking around Weaver for the next few months?

The thought was more than a little irritating. "Sam, you haven't met Justin Clay yet, have you? He's Erik's brother."

Sam turned her bright eyes back to Justin. "No kidding? You're the genius scientist who works back East." She stuck out her hand, cocking her blond head a little to one side. "I guess I see the resemblance to Erik," she said with a smile. "Except you're prettier."

Tabby nearly choked on her amusement when Justin flushed.

"He'd argue that," he said and nearly yanked back his hand from Sam's.

"Sam's one of Max's deputies," Tabby told him. "Like Sloan."

"Well, I wear a badge like Sloan," Sam allowed wryly. "But nobody calls me their boss like they do Sloan." She picked up the box of rolls. "Still warm. Wonder if Ruiz will mind if one is missing before I get them to him?"

"I'd like to see the day when you actually indulge yourself for once," Tabby challenged.

"Oh, I indulge." Sam's gaze sparkled as she glanced at Justin on her way toward the door.

"With a *sweet roll*," Tabby called after her.

Sam just laughed and sketched a wave as she left.

"Heard there was a lady deputy now," Justin said when the sound of the bell over the door faded. "She still the only one?"

"Max has been trying to recruit more women." Tabby picked up a rag and started needlessly polishing the counter. "It's hard. Small-town USA is bad enough. Small town in the middle of Wyoming—where the tumbleweeds often outnumber the residents—isn't the life for everyone." Her fingers clenched around the rag as she rubbed harder. "Not even when you're born and raised in it. You ought to know that better than anyone." He was the perfect example of getting out, after all. "So what's this big project you're doing? Curing the common cold?"

"Nothing that profitable. Just an R&D project that should've been wrapped up already, but—"

There was a loud bang from the back of the diner, followed by, "Yo, yo, yo!"

Justin shoved his fingers through his hair, looking impatient. "Now what?"

"Bubba," Tabby said evenly. "If you want peace and quiet, Ruby's Café isn't the place to find it. Why do you think those profit checks you get have a decent number of zeros at the end? Not that you probably notice them much, anyway, with your gigantic pharmaceutical salary." She pushed through the swinging door to greet her cook. "Morning, Bubba."

"Hey, girl." Bubba Bumble had a gentle soul that he hid behind a lumbering, rough-looking, hard-talking exterior. "Figured you'd have the hash browns going already." He was wrapping a white apron over his white T-shirt and slouchy, black-and-white-striped pants. Next came a pristine red-and-black bandanna that he wrapped over his forehead and tied in the back over his neatly shaved salt-and-pepper hair.

"Sorry. I got—" *Distracted by Justin.* "Busy," she said instead.

Bubba grunted and grabbed a knife to start peeling potatoes. Leaving him to it, she went back out front. The regular waitresses would begin arriving any minute, but until they did, she was on deck. Once they were there, though, she'd spend most of her morning in the kitchen with Bubba. She could man the grill when she had to, but he was the cook. She took care of the baking—he didn't like the ancient oven Tabby still used—and did the books and serving or kitchen prep when the load was heavy. And considering the pool tournament being held down the street, she was crossing her fingers for a heavy day.

She topped up Justin's coffee again without waiting for him to ask and began restocking the rack that held individual boxes of cold cereal.

"Does anyone still order those things?"

"Absolutely." She gave the rack a whirl. "Or did you think these were the same boxes of Fruity Twirls that were here when your great-grandma ran the place?"

He ignored her sarcasm.

"Since you're here, you might as well eat. Biscuits and gravy? Pancakes? Or have your tastes gotten fancier along with your running clothes?"

"If they had, I wouldn't be sitting on this stool," he replied with such an even tone that she felt guilty. "What's the special?"

She kept a small chalkboard propped on a shelf behind the counter where she listed the daily specials. But she hadn't gotten to writing them out yet today, and the board was still wiped clean, the way she'd left it two days earlier.

"Bubba," she called without looking behind her toward the pass-through window to the kitchen. "What's the special this morning?"

"Turkey hash," he yelled back. "Turkey noodle soup and salad this afternoon."

She retrieved the board and chalk and wrote everything out. She'd just set the board back in place when the front door opened and a couple she didn't know came in. They were both carrying long, distinctive cases. "Good morning," she greeted. "Looks like you're in town for the tournament. Sit anywhere you like. I'll be right over with menus." Without waiting a beat, she looked at Justin again. "So? What'll you have?"

"Scrambled eggs and wheat toast."

He liked eggs now? Withholding comment, she turned and leaned closer to the pass-through. "Scrambled eggs and wheat for Justin, Bubba."

Her cook looked up from the growing mountain of potatoes he'd shredded. "Justin's here?" He immediately set down his knife and crossed the kitchen to look through the pass-through. "Justin! How's life treating you, man?"

"It's good, Bubba. You?"

Ignoring their conversation, Tabby carried two waters and menus over to the couple, who'd chosen a booth in the corner. "I'm Tabby. Can I get you coffee or anything else besides water while you have a chance to look over the menu?"

"Bloody Mary?" The young woman looked hopeful.

Tabby smiled and shook her head. "Sorry. No alcohol here. Colbys will be able to accommodate you on that, though, if you have your heart set. You'll get a good breakfast there, too. Not as good as here—" she gave a quick wink "—but good all the same."

"I suppose I can live without one." The girl propped her chin on her hand. "What about you, honey?"

"Coffee's good for me. And one of those pecan cinnamon rolls that I keep hearing about." The man flipped open the menu.

"Oh, me, too." The girl's expression brightened. "And cream for my coffee if you've got it. It's a holiday weekend. If I can't splurge on a Bloody Mary just yet, I'll splurge on that."

Tabby's smile turned into a grin. "Coming right up."

Infinitely comfortable with this particular role, she returned to the counter area, prepared a little white jug of cold cream, plated up two warm rolls and returned with them, along with the coffeepot, to the table. While she was serving the couple, the door jingled again, and two more parties of two came in. Everyone had pool cue cases.

She hid her delight and called out another cheerful "Good morning."

She'd just gotten them situated with menus and drinks when Bubba called out that an order was up, and she went back to grab Justin's plate. Which also had a side of biscuits and gravy.

Bubba figured he knew Justin pretty well, too, obviously.

Tabby set his plate in front of him, and Justin eyed the fat, fluffy biscuit that was mounded over with golden-brown gravy studded with chunks of sausage. She reached below the counter and came up with a bottle of hot sauce. She was tempted to hold it out of his reach, but she set it in front of him. "Anything else I can get for you?" She lifted her eyebrows, waiting. "More coffee?"

"No coffee. But there is something else." He hesitated a moment, then suddenly dumped the biscuit and gravy on top of the eggs, completely hiding them, and grabbed the hot sauce.

She hid a smile as she pivoted on her heel to grab an order that Bubba set on the pass-through. "More gravy?"

"The key to the empty unit you've still got at the triplex," he said. "I want to rent it."

Chapter Four

Tabby turned and was staring at him as if he'd started speaking Swahili. "What's that?"

"You still have an empty unit at your triplex, don't you? Erik told me last night—"

"Yes," she said, looking consternated. "I haven't managed to rent out the third unit yet, but—"

"Well, now you have," he said, content to do his own share of interrupting. "At least for six weeks or so."

Her lips parted, and he knew she wanted to tell him no. He knew it. Just as he knew there was no way that she could. Their families were too close. Their moms were best friends. Her brother was married to one of his cousins.

She managed the diner he and his brother owned.

"I'll pay twice what you were planning to charge," he said in a low tone. "Just say okay, Tab, and neither one of us'll have to go around explaining why we're the only ones who don't think it's such a great idea. My family suggested it last night after you cut and ran."

"I didn't cut and run." Her lips twisted, and she looked away. The bell over the door jingled twice more in rapid succession. "Fine," she said abruptly. "Meet me over there at two this afternoon. I'll give you the key." Then she snatched two slick, laminated menus out of the slot next to the cash register and smiled almost maniacally at the newcomers. "Good morning!"

Justin wondered if he was the only one who heard the wealth of false cheer that had entered her voice.

He wished to hell he'd never admitted to Erik the night before that he wasn't exactly anxious to move back home for the next several weeks.

Not because he didn't love his folks. He did. But he'd been out on his own for a long time, and he was used to having his own space. One where his mother didn't figure she ought to make up his bed every morning.

If he hadn't made that admission to Erik, then Izzy wouldn't have overheard, and then his mom wouldn't have come in on the conversation. Hope hadn't been insulted at all, either. In fact, she'd been the one to toss out ideas for places he might rent temporarily. Erik, though, had been the one to remember Tabby's place.

And wasn't that just the perfect solution?

Everyone knew Justin and Tabby were friends. Always had been. *Thick as thieves.* That's how his mom had put it as she'd reminisced.

He wasn't about to tell them those days were over. That Tabby would just as soon kick him to the edge of town than agree to rent one of her triplex units to him. And he definitely wasn't about to tell them the reason why.

He dumped more hot sauce on the sausage gravy.

And when he was finished, it was one of the waitresses—a girl he didn't know named Paulette—who took away his half-empty plate.

* * *

Tabby spotted the dusty black pickup truck parked in front of her triplex the second she rounded the corner of her street.

She wanted to turn on her heel and go back to the safety of the diner. Justin might be half owner, but at least there she figured she was safe from him showing up again that day.

Huffing out a breath, she tucked her chin inside the turned-up collar of her coat and trudged forward. When she got closer, she saw that he was sitting on her front porch. He'd changed into jeans and a light gray hoodie.

The cigarette dangling between his fingers wasn't such a welcome sight. He stubbed it out when he spotted her and rubbed his hands down his thighs as he stood, waiting for her to walk closer. But the faint smell of smoke lingered.

"When'd you start smoking again?" He'd smoked for a few years in grad school. Never around his folks. And rarely around her. And she knew he'd worked like a dog to give up the habit. Because what good was a guy researching cancer cures who died of it himself?

He frowned. "I haven't started up again."

She pointedly pushed the toe of her boot against the cigarette butt sitting on the edge of her cement porch.

"I've been working on the same pack for weeks."

She looked at him from the corner of her eye as she passed him to unlock the front door of her unit. "Question is why you have a pack of cigarettes at all."

"I know. Disgusting habit. Unhealthy as hell."

All of which was true.

So why, darn it, had there been something so stupidly sexy about him sitting there with one?

It was insane.

Maybe it went along with that whole bad-boy appeal thing.

Not that Justin had ever been a bad boy.

He'd just been the boy who got away.

She pushed open the door. "You coming in or going to stand there and wait while I find the key for the empty unit?" It was pretty much an excuse. She knew where the key was. She just wasn't all that anxious to hand it over to him.

But then, she wasn't all that anxious to have him inside her home, either. As it was, she thought about him often enough without him ever having stepped foot inside.

He bent over and retrieved the crumpled cigarette butt and stepped through her doorway, pushing the door closed behind him. "Trash?"

She gestured to the kitchen, which was separated from the living room by only a bat-wing-shaped breakfast bar. "Under the sink." She chewed the inside of her cheek, watching him cross the room. "The empty unit is on the other end. Floor plan's just like mine. Two bedrooms. Fireplace. One bath. Furnished, which I assume you heard. Minimally, though, so don't expect all the comforts you're used to. You've got a utility room, but no washer and dryer." And she'd be hanged if she would offer the use of hers. He had plenty of family around Weaver he could ask, and if not them, then there was a brand-new Laundromat out on the other side of town by Shop-World.

"I don't care what the floor plan is or whether there's a washer and dryer. I don't know what luxuries you figure I've got in Boston. I don't have a washer and dryer there, either. Long as it has running water and electricity, I'm good. What prompted you to buy this place?"

She raised her shoulders, a little thrown by the abrupt question. "I don't know."

He gave her a look.

She pressed her lips together. "Fine. With all the new building going on at the other end of town, some of these old places are starting to go vacant. The original owner—do you remember Mr. Samuelson? He had that bait-and-tackle shack—" She made herself stop rambling. "Anyway, he died. Had no family. There was talk about an investor who wanted to buy this lot and the house next door, but only to raze them and put up a convenience store."

He grimaced.

"Right. That was my reaction, too. Plenty of new building going on at the other end of town. But downtown here? It's charming just the way it is. Anyway," she hurried on, skipping the rest of her reasons, "it's close enough to work that I can usually walk."

"Like you did today."

"Obviously."

"Even though when you walk *to* work, it's early. And pitch-dark."

"So?"

He sighed. "Christ, Tabby. That's practically the middle of the night. You shouldn't be out walking—"

"—the three very short blocks in this town where nothing ever happens?"

"Why didn't you charge Sloan McCray this morning for his coffee and roll? It's not because he works for the sheriff's department. You charged that blonde lady deputy for hers."

Tabby clamped her lips shut. The fact that he'd asked told her that he already knew.

"He busted a guy who was trying to rob the diner, that's why." Justin pressed his hands flat on the granite-topped breakfast bar and stared at her. "Yeah, I asked and heard all about it. He busted in. While you were there. Alone before hours. With the damned door unlocked."

"And for a year after it happened, I *kept* the door locked," she snapped. "Until I got tired of having to stop what I was doing and go unlock it every time I turned around, because half this town knows I'm there long before six when the place officially opens and stops by, anyway!"

"You need to be more careful."

"I locked my house door, didn't I?" She realized she was yelling and let out a long breath. "I'll get your key," she muttered and hurried down the hall.

She used the spare room as a studio and office. She found the key in the bottom of an empty coffee can that also held her clean paintbrushes and returned to the living room.

He was still standing in the kitchen, and she set the key on the granite. "There you go. Rent's due in advance." She blamed the devil for prompting her to make that up right then and there.

He spread his hands. "Not exactly packing a checkbook here, Tab."

"The bank's open until five. But you'll have to park a few blocks away because of the traffic in town for the pool tournament."

He sighed a little and pocketed the key. "Who lives in the middle unit?"

"Mrs. Wachowski. She used to teach history at the high school—"

"I remember her. She was ancient when we were in school. Surprised she's still around. She must be a hundred and twenty by now."

Tabby didn't want to feel amusement over anything he said, but the retired teacher *had* seemed ancient when they were teenagers. And she would have been totally displaced, just like Mr. Rowe, who was seventy and lived in the house next door, if someone hadn't purchased the triplex. "She's eighty-five. And she's very nice, but she's a light sleeper. So if you're still prone to blasting old Van Halen when you can't sleep, be aware."

"I played it when I studied," he corrected her. "And it was AC/DC. Not Van Halen."

"Whatever." She was blithely dismissive. As if she didn't remember very well what it had actually been. She went to the door and opened it. "Don't forget the bank."

He crossed the room and stopped in front of her, so close she could see the faint lines radiating from his violet eyes. "I don't forget anything."

Her palm felt slippery clenched around the doorknob. "You forgot we were friends," she said huskily.

"I didn't forget that, either."

Her throat went tight, and she damned the sudden burning she could feel behind her eyes. "Fine. Whatever." She just wanted him to go.

"Tabby—"

She clenched her jaw.

He sighed. Shook his head slightly. "I'll bring you the rent money later."

She nodded stoically.

He sighed again and stepped through the door. She barely waited for him to get through before she pushed it closed after him.

Then she leaned back against it and let out a shaking breath.

He remembered her name now.

Maybe if he'd remembered it that night they'd slept together, she wouldn't feel the way she did now.

But no. That night four years ago, after he'd peeled off her clothing as if he'd been unwrapping something exquisitely precious and pulled her into his arms, taking her virginity and her heart in one fell swoop, he hadn't remembered her name at all.

It hadn't been Tabby's name he'd whispered against her skin.

It had been Gillian's.

That night, Justin stuck the rent check in an envelope and shoved it through the mail slot in Tabby's front door.

Call him a coward, but he didn't think he had the stomach to go another round with her.

Instead, he'd killed the evening at Colbys, the bar and grill owned by his cousin Casey's new wife, Jane. It had been crowded as hell there, what with the tournament going strong. But since several of the participants were relatives of his, he'd managed to slide his way in. During a break in the play, he'd thrown darts with Caleb and April. He'd tilted beers with JD and argued politics with Jake.

He'd also spent nearly an hour on the phone with Charles, convincing his boss that helping to fill the hospital's shortfall in funds for their lab expansion was an investment worth making if CNJ wanted Justin to successfully bring the results of their latest research project in on time.

It hadn't been Justin's project in the first place. It wasn't even in his usual area of research, which was cancer treatments. Though even before this latest issue, Justin seemed to keep getting pulled farther and farther from the lab.

But Charles had dumped the matter in his lap only a week ago, when the guy who *had* been in charge of it had been arrested on drug charges. Not only was Charles trying to minimize the scandal of that, but he needed the final report on the project to be ready for presentation at a conference in Europe right after New Year's. CNJ was small potatoes in the pharma world. But with this report, Justin's boss expected major results.

If the report was completed on time.

If the results of the project were even accurate. Which was what Justin had yet to prove, considering the situation.

Five weeks to accomplish something that usually took five months. Sometimes five years.

Was it any wonder he'd wanted to get away from Boston and the pressure of his own responsibilities in the lab there? Much less the pain in the butt Gillian had been making of herself.

Key in hand, he walked along the sidewalk fronting all three of the connected units to the door at the opposite end. It was dark, but there was a porch light on, so he had no trouble fitting the key in the lock, and the door swung open with only a slight creak of the hinges.

He stepped inside and felt around for a light switch on the wall but couldn't find one. Swearing under his breath, he pushed the door wider so that the light from the porch could extend inside and felt his way into the pitch-dark interior.

His knee connected with something hard and solid, and he swore loudly, reaching out to feel his way around it.

A couch. Which hopefully led to a side table and a lamp.

Why the *hell* hadn't he checked the place out while it was still daylight?

Tabby was why.

He reached the end of the couch and cautiously felt around for a side table. He nearly knocked the lamp over when he found it, but finally, he felt the switch and turned it.

The resulting light nearly scorched his eyeballs.

He blinked and looked away, going back to the door to close it. It was cold outside and nearly as cold inside the apartment. He looked over the living area. It was definitely a twin to Tabby's place. At least in layout.

The furnishings were a lot sparer. The couch looked like standard-issue hotel stuff, making him wonder where she'd gotten it. The simple side table and the lamp were straight out of the '80s. Not that he cared. He didn't plan to spend a lot of time here, anyway.

He just hoped the bed was big enough to stretch out on and comfortable enough to allow him a night's sleep.

He found the thermostat on the wall in the hallway and turned on the heat, then checked out the two bedrooms. They were identical except one was outfitted with twin beds—which was never gonna work, since he was six foot four—and the other had a queen-size bed. Not perfect, but doable.

Only thing it was missing was the bed linens.

He looked in the closets, which were all empty except for little cedar blocks that hung from hanger poles. He found nothing in the dresser drawers, either.

Evidently, the term *furnished* only went so far.

He went out to the truck he'd borrowed from the Double-C for the duration of his stay and retrieved the suitcase holding his clothes. He left the other two suitcases containing the research materials locked inside the cab of the truck. Tomorrow he'd take them to the hospital, where his aunt had promised him some dedicated lab and office space that, truthfully, she hadn't had to agree to. He was glad that she had, though, even though it would cost CNJ a nice chunk of change.

Maybe he was glad *because* it would cost CNJ a nice chunk of change. It made up, just a little, for the chaos his life had become there.

CNJ had millions to throw around. The Weaver Hospital—which served this entire region of Wyoming—didn't.

It didn't take him long to unpack. There wasn't any need here for the suits and ties he typically wore to work in Boston on those days he wasn't suited up in scrubs. He also hadn't bothered bringing his heavy coat, just a few sweatshirts and his leather jacket. He figured if he needed something heavier, he'd borrow it from Erik or his dad.

And if he was honest with himself, it had felt good leaving that stuff behind. Stuff that Gillian had always had a hand in choosing, only because he'd never been interested in it himself.

The contents of his suitcase took up a third of the

bedroom closet and one of the dresser drawers. He dumped his shaving kit on the bathroom counter.

The heater was running steadily, filling the cold air with a faint, burning odor that he figured would dissipate after an hour or two. From the smell, he doubted that the heater had been used in months.

He went out to the kitchen to verify he had running water. He did. Hot and cold, even. He pulled open a few drawers and cabinet doors. He hadn't been able to find any bed linens. But there were dishes. A few pots and pans. Silverware. All clean and neatly stacked in their various spots. Next, he checked the refrigerator. It was cold inside, with only an opened box of baking soda occupying space on one of the shelves.

With a mental list forming of the basics he could pick up out at Shop-World, he left the apartment again and headed out to the truck. He couldn't help looking toward Tabby's place at the other end.

Despite the late hour, light was shining through the closed curtains over her front window.

He wondered if she was really awake this late when he knew she'd have been at the restaurant since around 4:00 a.m.

Even as he was looking, he saw the curtains twitch. A moment later, her front door opened, and for a moment she stood there, silhouetted by the light.

Then the door closed, and she was heading toward him, little more than a dark shadow against the darker night.

"Here," she said, stopping a few feet away. She extended her hand. She was holding a square, plastic-covered package. "I meant to put them in your place earlier, but I fell asleep on the couch. It's a new set of bedsheets."

He took the package. "Thanks. One less thing to pick up at Shop-World."

"That's where you're heading?"

"Somewhere else to go at eleven o'clock at night?" It was also the only place close by where a person could pick up bedsheets, a set of mattresses to put them on, pajamas to wear when you lay down on them and food to cook when you got up again. There was nothing fancy about the big store, but it did have its purpose around these parts.

She was shifting from one foot to the other and back again. Her hair was darker than dark, but he still imagined he could see the gleam of her eyes in the thin moonlight. He thought he caught a whisper of a smile on her lips. "Colbys, particularly when there's a pool tournament going on."

"Already spent enough time there for one day." He was surprised she'd given him the sheets, much less remained there, voluntarily speaking with him about anything at all. "Look, Tabby." He gestured with the package. "I appreciate the place. I know you'd have rather—"

She cut her hand through the space between them. "Let's just not talk about it. For everyone's sake, we can pretend everything's hunky-dory. Same way we've done when you've been in town before."

Pretending for several weeks would be harder than pretending for a few hours. But he wasn't going to look a gift horse in the mouth. "So. Truce?"

She laughed. The sound was soft. And entirely unamused. "Pretense doesn't mean truce, Justin. But I love your family as much as I love my own. Just because you and I—" She moistened her lips and shifted restlessly. "They all think we're still the same kids who played together in the sandbox. That belief makes them happy, and I see no reason to rock that boat. Particularly when there's enough of that going on with your family already."

"What's *that* supposed to mean?"

She exhaled. "Your grandfather's reaction to Vivian Templeton moving to town."

"Oh. That." He raked his fingers through his hair. "Erik mentioned it." Frankly, he failed to see what the fuss was about. There'd always been a lot of Clays on the family tree. Now there was just another branch they'd never known about before. It was hardly the end of the world.

"Anyway, it's not like we have to sit down to a holiday meal with everyone every day. So—" she crossed her arms and shrugged "—you'll go your way and I'll go mine. We'll hardly see each other. And before we know it, this'll all be over. You'll go back to Boston and Gillian." She started to turn away.

"Not Gillian."

Tabby looked back at him. Her skin was as creamy as the cameo his mother had let him play with during church when he was a kid so he'd sit still in the pew.

"She's not part of my life anymore," he said bluntly. "We broke up. For good this time." He wasn't sure what reaction he expected. But he did know it wasn't the musing little "hmm" he got. "Six months ago," he added for good measure.

"She's still your boss's daughter?"

He didn't answer. Obviously, Gillian was still Charles's daughter.

Tabby wasn't done, though. "You're still both working at CNJ?" She started walking toward her doorway. "Then she's not out of your life," she said without looking back.

Justin opened his mouth to argue, but he didn't.

Tabby reached her door. Opened it and disappeared inside. A moment later, the light shining through her curtains was extinguished.

He stood there in the dark for a long while, listening to the silence.

In Boston, where he had a dinky apartment with an exorbitant rent in the South End, there was never such a wealth of silence.

He'd always thought that was a good thing. Everything about Boston had energized him. The city. Grad school. His work. His tumultuous relationship with Gillian.

He looked up at the sky. It was mostly cloudy, allowing only a stingy stream of moonlight. But on a clear night, he knew the stars would be laid out like a thick, sparkling carpet.

When they'd been young, he, Tabby and Caleb had often camped out behind her parents' house. They'd pitch a tent and everything, though they usually ended up pulling their sleeping bags out of the tent. They'd fall asleep under the stars, amid ghost stories and trying to figure out the constellations.

Caleb had been the best at identifying them. Tabby's artistic eye had usually seen something else in the stars— a bunch of dancing fairies and such.

Justin had seen cities. And skyscrapers.

Even then, he'd been thinking about someplace else. A place where everyone in town didn't know the name of everyone else in town. And certainly didn't know their business. Where a person could walk down the street in complete anonymity if he wanted. Where tumbleweeds didn't travel down the center of Main Street more frequently than cars.

He shook the thoughts out of his head.

Then he unlocked his truck, tossed the bedsheets onto the bench seat beside him and drove out to Shop-World.

He could have survived a night without sheets. But in the morning, he was gonna need coffee. And even though he had ample justification to stop by the café to get a cup on his way to the hospital—they were spitting distance from one another, practically—he figured he and Tabby both would be better off if he gave Ruby's a wide berth.

At least for a while.

Chapter Five

On Monday, Tabby dragged the box of Christmas decorations out of storage and turned the radio station to one that played only holiday music.

It would drive some of her customers a little bananas at first. But after a week or so, they'd be humming along with the music, too.

She was hoping that the decorations and the music would immediately put her in a more cheerful state of mind. Ordinarily, once she got past the hurdle of Justin's brief Thanksgiving visit, she would throw herself into the Christmas spirit. She was determined that this year was going to be no different.

Even if the hurdle happened to be a living, breathing obstacle temporarily residing all but next door to her.

So what if her humming along with "White Christmas" sounded a little manic? She was the only one who knew the reason why.

By the time Bubba arrived and fired up the grill, she had green garland strung around all of the windows. By noon, she'd rearranged a few of the tables to accommodate the Christmas tree. It wasn't a live tree; she didn't want to have to deal with needles dropping on the floor in the restaurant. But it was a nice artificial one all the same. And by the time she closed up again at two, everyone had had a hand in decorating it. Even some of her customers had pitched in.

And the Christmas tunes she was humming had become a little less frantic sounding, even to her own critical ears.

It probably helped that Justin hadn't shown his face at the diner. Not that she'd expected him to, but still.

She left the locking-up duties to Bubba and walked the till from that day and the weekend over to the bank to deposit.

Then, considering it *was* officially the Christmas shopping season, she stopped in one of her favorite shops, Classic Charms, to see if anything struck her fancy. She figured she'd run into either Sydney or Tara, who owned the eclectic shop. But neither one was there. The cash register was being manned by a teenage girl Tabby didn't know.

Tabby's mother, Jolie, however, was browsing the racks.

"Honey!" Jolie smiled broadly and hastily tucked a hanger back on the circular rack of clothes. "I didn't expect to see you here."

"Same goes." Tabby gave her mom a quick hug and tried to spy what she'd been looking at. "Thought I'd get a start on Christmas gifts. What was that you were looking at? Anything good?"

Jolie gave the rack a whirl. "This place is full of many good things," she said, smiling serenely and almost evasively. "I just came from lunch with Hope. Why didn't you tell me Justin was staying at your place?"

Tabby's smile felt suddenly wooden. "He's renting the empty unit." *Staying at her place* had an entirely different connotation, as far as she was concerned. "Just wants somewhere to crash while he works on some project. Haven't seen much of him, actually."

"Well, that won't last," Jolie said with certainty. "Bring him by for dinner this week. Your dad and I would love to see him."

"I think he's got a lot of work—" The words died when her mom gave her a curious look. Tabby knew the more she made excuses, the more curious Jolie Taggart would likely become. "But I'm sure he'd take a break for you guys," she finished.

"Wonderful." Jolie glanced around the shop. "Now, we could both save a lot of time and effort if we just told each other what in here we've had our eye on."

Tabby couldn't help but chuckle. "Yes. But where would be the fun in that?"

Her mother sighed dramatically. "You are your father's daughter." She glanced at her watch and made a face. "I'd stay and pump you for gift ideas, but I'm meeting a new client this afternoon."

"Designing another wedding dress?" Her mother was a seamstress, and in the last several years, wedding dresses had seemed to be one of her most frequent requests.

Jolie shook her head. "A ball gown, actually." She glanced around the shop that sold bits of everything from clothing to furniture. "She doesn't want it getting around before she sends out invitations, but Vivian Templeton is planning a Christmas party. It's a little short notice, but she asked me to make her gown."

"Flattering."

"I thought so. Heaven knows the woman could hire any designer in the world if she felt like it. I was surprised she didn't request Izzy, though. When it comes to doing the fancy stuff, she's a lot better at it."

Before moving with Murphy to Weaver, Izzy had been the costume designer for a ballet company based in New York. She'd waited tables for Tabby for a while, and she'd been a good worker. But designing clothing was clearly more up her alley, and since she'd helped Jolie out with one particularly difficult bride, the two of them had done several more jobs together.

"Izzy's married to Erik, though," Tabby reasoned. "Maybe Vivian was trying to be sensitive to the fact that she's part of the Clay family."

Jolie tucked a runaway curl of blond hair behind her ear and pursed her lips. "Possibly. Hope and I were talking about all that over lunch. She says Squire's more adamant than ever about having nothing to do with Vivian.

"Obviously I never knew Squire's first wife, Sarah, since she died before I was even born. But Vivian was Sarah's sister-in-law. I know she interfered somehow and prevented her husband from having any sort of relationship with Sarah, but that was years ago. You know that old man is all about family. And learning now that there's a passel of them living practically under his nose ought to count for something."

Tabby frowned. "I hadn't heard that Squire wasn't willing to acknowledge the family connection at all."

Jolie waved her hand dismissively. "I wouldn't go that far. But he's sure got a grudge, and is dead set against meeting Vivian face-to-face. Evidently, she's asked him several times, but he flatly refuses."

"They all seemed okay when I was over there for

Thanksgiving dinner. Of course, nobody mentioned Vivian's name within his earshot, either. At least not while I was there." A customer came in, and Tabby slowly twirled the display rack. There was a goldish-brown blouse she spotted that exactly matched the color of her mom's eyes, and as soon as her mother left, she planned to get a closer look at it.

"Well, the only thing I know directly from Vivian herself is that she's planning a formal party the weekend before Christmas," Jolie said in a low voice. "And now I'm going to have to hurry, or I'm going to be late." She bussed Tabby's cheek and headed for the front door. "Let me know what night you're bringing Justin by," she said as she left.

Tabby's shoulders sank. She'd *almost* managed to forget that particular request.

She pulled the hanger off the rack and looked at the pretty blouse. It would suit her mother very well.

But Tabby's spurt of holiday shopping spirit had abruptly dissipated, and she replaced the hanger.

She didn't have to examine the reason why.

Justin.

The office space his aunt was able to allot for him at the hospital lab was considerably smaller than what he was used to, but Justin didn't care. He had room for all materials he had to go through, a safe to lock them in and a lock on the door. Not that he was particularly worried about industrial espionage. Not in Weaver.

But he knew stranger things had happened.

So when he finally left the office late that Monday night, he packed up his laptop to take with him, closed the research logs in the safe and locked the door behind him.

"Finally heading out?" Scott Brown, the only lab tech on duty that night, barely glanced up from his microscope.

"Yeah." Justin slid his laptop into his messenger bag and slung the strap over his shoulder. He didn't know much else about the technician besides the guy's name. "When do you get off?"

"Two o'clock in the morning." Scott replaced the slide he was studying with another. He looked about Justin's age. Maybe a few years older. "Hate the swing shift, but I like the extra pay that comes with it." He tapped his foot on the metal rung of his high stool to the beat of the country music coming from a radio sitting on one of the steel shelves lining the walls. Walls that would be opened up soon, effectively tripling the current space.

Justin stopped at the locked door that controlled access to the lab and signed out. "You're not originally from around here, are you?"

"Braden."

Weaver's nearest neighbor. A good thirty miles away. It wasn't as if there were any handy public transportation methods around. No subway. No commuter train. And maybe the drive wouldn't be considered that much of a commute to some, but it was only a two-lane highway that got you there and back.

When the weather was good and there were no accidents or semitrucks to slow you down, the trip wasn't difficult. But when the snow and ice came?

Different story.

"Don't envy you that," Justin said and lifted his hand before leaving.

Even though his borrowed truck was in the parking lot, Justin could have walked from the hospital back to Tabby's.

It was no farther than walking to the diner from the triplex.

Knowing that she did so—regularly—annoyed the hell out of him. Weaver was still a small town, yes. But it wasn't the same small town in which they'd grown up.

The streets weren't the same streets where they'd raced around on their bicycles when they were ten. These days, you were just as likely to encounter a stranger on the street as you were a person you'd known your entire life. And a weekend pool tournament like the one his cousin-in-law had just thrown didn't have to be going on to draw strangers to town.

These days, strangers were actually *moving* to town.

He dumped his messenger bag on the passenger seat and headed home. His cell phone buzzed before he got there. Half the time, the cell service didn't work around Weaver, so he was surprised enough that he glanced at the display.

The sight of Gillian's name had him grimacing. He silenced the thing, not answering, and shoved the phone into the messenger bag. Two minutes later, he turned onto Tabby's street and parked in the driveway next to a gunboat of a vehicle left over from a dozen decades ago. Mrs. Wachowski's, no doubt.

He wasn't sure if Tabby still drove the sporty little coupe she'd had years ago. He hadn't seen it around. But he also hadn't seen any other car he could peg as hers, either.

When he got to his front door, there was a piece of paper taped to it, and he peeled it off and unfolded it.

Tabby's handwriting was as illegible as it always had been. For a girl who'd been able to draw circles around his stick figures from way back, she'd always had the most atrocious penmanship. And no amount of trying was going to help him decipher the scratchings. He was too far out of practice.

He went inside long enough to dump off the messenger bag, then walked down to her door and knocked.

And knocked.

And knocked.

He'd given up and was turning to go back to his place when the door finally squeaked open and Tabby stood there, several paintbrushes threaded through the fingers of one hand. Her hair was haphazardly pinned on top of her head in a messy knot, and she had a smear of red paint on her cheek.

"Looks like you still throw yourself entirely into your painting," he said and swiped his thumb over the dab of paint, holding it up to show her.

She tossed the rag that was hanging over the shoulder of her misshapen T-shirt at him. "If your plumbing's stopped up, call a plumber."

"Nice landlady you make."

She made a face at him and turned on her bare foot. "Come in and close the door. You're letting out the heat. I suppose you're here about the note," she said, heading out of the living room.

He wiped the paint off his thumb and pushed the door closed with his shoulder before following her. "Since I could only make out about three words of it, yeah." He stopped in the doorway of the bedroom she'd en-

tered and stared. "Damn, Tabby." There seemed to be
dozens of paintings stacked up against the walls. Large
canvases. Small canvases. And every size in between.
"Do you paint instead of sleep these days?"

"Sometimes," she muttered. She'd sat down on a
tall wooden stool in front of her easel positioned near
the window but remained facing him. She took up another rag from a stack of them and started cleaning her
brushes. "Any night'll work."

He tilted the nearest stack of paintings away from
the wall so he could look through them. They were
all abstracts. "Looks like Jackson Pollock and Georgia
O'Keeffe had a baby." He glanced at her. "Any night'll
work for what?"

She turned to set aside her brushes on her worktable,
and her T-shirt slipped off one shoulder. "Dinner. Did
you read the note or not?"

He tossed the note next to her brushes. "It's harder
to figure out than your paintings."

"My mom expects me to bring you around for dinner
this week. I couldn't come up with a good reason to tell
her no." She folded her arms across her chest. She was
wearing narrow blue jeans with stains and rips on them
that he knew came from years of use rather than some
deliberate fashion style. She had one knee bent to prop
her foot on the base of the revolving stool and one leg
stretched out in front of her, and her toes were painted
as brilliantly red as the smear he'd wiped off her cheek.

Over the years, he'd noticed lots of things about her,
but he couldn't remember ever really noticing her toes.
They were decidedly…cute.

Shaking off the thought, he started looking through
another stack of paintings. "I don't care what night. Just

pick and get it over with." He lifted the canvas closest to the wall to look more closely at it. "Reminds me of a blizzard. Remember that time we got stuck at the high school during that February blizzard?" Twenty kids and one adult, sleeping on gym mats in the auditorium with no lights or electricity.

The corners of her lips barely lifted in acknowledgment. "How about Wednesday? Six o'clock. If you can manage an hour, I'm sure they'll be satisfied. We probably won't have to play this charade again until Christmas Eve."

When his family had always gone to her folks' place after church. When they'd been kids, they'd all bedded down together in the basement, whispering about what Santa might bring, while upstairs, they could hear their parents laughing.

"Wednesday's fine." He lowered the painting back in place and carefully leaned the canvases once more against the wall. "Do you sell them all?"

"Most of them." She clasped the round seat beneath her. "Bolieux sells them, anyway."

"That the gallery Sydney got you hooked up with?"

"Mmm-hmm." She spread her fingers and looked at her fingernails. Picked at some dried paint. "Once I ship all of these to them, they'll display and catalog them. List them online, too. I've sold a lot more since they started doing that."

"You getting good money for them?"

"Not enough to buy Ruby's yet, but I'm getting there."

He stopped in his tracks.

She raised her eyebrows. "What? You find that surprising?"

"I don't know. I never thought about it. Does Erik know about this?"

"I've mentioned it a time or two in passing." She shrugged, and the shirt slipped down her shoulder another inch. It was clear that she wasn't wearing a bra. At least not one with straps.

He shook himself again. Why the *hell* was he noticing stuff like that? He'd worked damn hard over the years, training himself to overlook such things where she was concerned.

"Until I started making some money with my art," she continued, "it's just been a nice thought."

"Tabby's Café," he mused. He wasn't sure whether he liked the idea or not. It was as unsettling as thinking she had cute toes.

But she shook her head. "I wouldn't change the name. The place is Ruby's. Always has been. Always will be. At least as long as I have any input on the matter." She pushed off the stool and slipped past him through the doorway. "Wednesday at six. You s'pose they'll think it's odd when we don't drive out there together?"

Her parents lived outside town on a small spread where her dad still trained cutting horses. He found his gaze dragging over the stack of paintings containing the one with the blizzard-like blue, gray and white swirls. "Uh, yeah." He went after her. "They'd think it was odd."

She'd gone into her kitchen and pulled open the refrigerator door. Unlike the plain white model in his unit, her stainless steel one looked brand-new. So did the coordinating range and the built-in microwave.

"So what're we going to do?" She took out a diet soda

and pulled the tab. It was obvious she wasn't going to offer him one.

"Drive out there together."

She turned her head around, as though she had a pain in her neck.

Of course, he was pretty certain his presence *was* the pain.

"Tell me again why you couldn't do this oh-so-important work of yours in Boston?"

Her T-shirt had slipped off her shoulder again.

He turned away from the sight and headed for the door. "Too many distractions there. I'll drive on Wednesday." His voice was abrupt. "Like you said. We'll probably be safe after that until Christmas Eve."

They weren't safe.

Two nights later, Tabby stared out the passenger window of Justin's truck as they drove back into Weaver from her parents' place.

What was supposed to have taken only an hour or so—just long enough to politely eat and run—had ended up consuming the entire evening. Mostly because Jolie had invited Tabby's brother and his family to join them.

The only saving grace was that Evan and Leandra's three kids—Hannah, Katie and Lucas—had kept the spotlight off Tabby and Justin.

And the fact that they'd barely exchanged five words even though they'd sat next to each other at the dinner table.

"Hannah looked good." Justin's voice broke the monotonous sound of the tires on the highway. Who knew how long ago the radio in the borrowed ranch truck had stopped working.

"She's comfortable at Mom and Dad's." Her eleven-year-old niece had autism. "She would have had a harder time with the whole crew at your folks' place on Thanksgiving. That's one of the reasons why Evan and Leandra tend to go see Helen in Gillette." Helen was her dad's stepmother. She was a difficult woman, to say the least. She had always been kind enough to Tabby, but the older she'd gotten, the less she appreciated Helen's attitude toward Jolie. Even after all these years, Jolie and Helen's relationship was strained.

"Your grandmother still dote on Evan?"

"To his chagrin, yes."

"He, uh, ever see—"

She knew where he was going. "Darian?" Her father's half brother was Evan's biological father, though he'd never spent one minute of his life acting like one. That had always been the role Drew Taggart held. He'd met Tabby's mom when she'd been pregnant with Evan, and they'd been married ever since. "No. Not for years, far as I know." It wasn't the only twist in her family tree, but given what was going on with the Clays and Templetons, it seemed mild in comparison. At least to her.

To her it was easy. Jolie and Drew were her parents. Evan was her brother. End of story, as far as she was concerned.

They fell silent, and she listened to the roll of the tires for a few more minutes. But it felt as if those tires were connected to a string that kept pulling tighter and tighter until she couldn't bear the silence another second.

"I didn't know they were going to bring up the tree

lighting," she said abruptly. "It never occurred to me. You're never here for it and—"

"It's not the end of the world."

She finally turned her head and looked at him.

The only light came from the occasional headlights of an oncoming vehicle. But even though she felt that he'd become a stranger these past few years, his features were forever imprinted in her mind.

"It's just one more time when our families are going to be together and we're going to have to keep pretending everything is hunky-dory between us." The tree-lighting ceremony was a town affair, scheduled for the coming Friday, just two days away.

She'd always enjoyed the festivity.

Now, the entire idea of it made her want to climb into bed and pull the covers over her head.

Could she do that until January without anyone noticing?

Inside her brain, she let out a frantic laugh.

"Well, maybe things *would* go back to being hunky-dory if you'd just let the past go." He slowed suddenly and pulled the truck off onto the shoulder of the highway, shoved it into Park and looked at her. "It was a *mistake*, Tabby."

"You got that right," she said tightly.

He exhaled noisily and shoved his fingers through his hair. "Okay, not a mistake. An accident. Do you think I intended—" He broke off again and swore under his breath. "I never meant to hurt you. I didn't mean to—"

"Call out another woman's name while you were caught in the throes of passion?" She filled her voice with sarcasm, because it was so much more preferable than letting the pain she still felt show.

"Yes!" He slammed his hand against the steering wheel, making her jump.

Then his wide shoulders rose and fell. "Yes," he repeated quietly. "I was drunk, Tab. You and I were *both* drunk. I was home, celebrating getting my PhD. Gillian and I were on the outs. Again. And you were my best friend. I didn't plan to get you into bed. I didn't plan any of that. It just…just happened."

It felt like a noose was tightening around her throat, and her eyes stung.

And when he spoke again, his voice was as ragged as she knew her own would have been. "And I know none of it excuses anything." His long fingers closed over her arm, squeezing. "D'you think I haven't regretted everything? That I haven't kicked myself every damned time I turn around? I'm sorry. I'm sorry. A hundred million times, I'm sorry. Just—" He cleared his throat. "Just tell me what I can do to make it right again, and I'll do it."

Did he regret making love with her? Or did he regret calling her by another woman's name?

Or was it the entire humiliating fiasco that he wished away?

Her throat felt raw. "It's not something that can be made right, Justin."

He exhaled. Squeezed her arm. "You haven't done anything in your life that you wished like hell you could take back? That you could undo?"

She closed her eyes, and a hot tear escaped. "Yes."

She wished she could undo falling in love with him. But she'd done that when she was about fifteen years old, when they'd been stuck together in the high school auditorium during a blizzard.

And she'd long ago given up hoping that she'd get over it.

"Then you understand," he said huskily. "I know you can't forget it. But you're one of the best people I've ever known, Tab. Can't you find some way to forgive?"

Yes, she could forgive.

But for years now, ever since he'd gone off to college and had never really come back, she'd had to watch him leave.

Again and again and again.

And in January, she'd watch him one more time.

So after the debacle four years ago, it had just been easier to hold on to the anger that resulted. And now, she wasn't sure if she could actually let it go. Even if she tried.

His fingers were hard and hot on her arm. Insistently reminding her that right now, right *now*, he was here.

"Fine," she whispered and felt something hard inside her chest start to give. A little. "It's over. In the past."

He waited a moment. Even in the shadows, she could feel the intensity of his gaze. "You forgive me?"

She inhaled deeply. Let her breath out slowly. Her tight shoulders sank.

"Yes. I forgive you."

Chapter Six

When Justin showed up at Ruby's before she'd unlocked the door at six, she realized he was determined to
make sure she'd meant her words from the night before.

He'd always been determined that way. And she'd
always been one to stand by her word.

So she unlocked the front door and threw her arm
wide in invitation. "Scrambled eggs?" Her tone was
dulcet.

The lines beside his violet eyes crinkled. His hair
was damp, and he smelled like heaven when he walked
past her.

"G'morning to you, too." He crossed to the counter
and dumped his messenger bag on a stool before sitting
down. "And you know I hate eggs."

She chewed the inside of her cheek, trying not to
laugh and failing.

And laughing, honestly laughing, with Justin felt too
good to regret. Even though she knew the opportunity
to do so came with an expiration date. "I knew you ordered those the other day just to be contrary." Some
things about him hadn't changed.

"Fortunately, Bubba's sausage gravy helped cover the taste. Mostly." He leaned over the counter to grab the coffeepot, and she quickly looked away from the sight of his faded blue jeans hugging his very perfect rear end. He didn't have quite the brawn that his cattle-ranching brother possessed, but there wasn't a single inch of Justin Clay that wasn't lean and oh so prime.

She didn't want to get caught ogling his butt and quickly went behind the counter to finish filling the saltshakers, which she'd been doing when he'd knocked on the glass door.

"So what are you going to be doing at the hospital today?" The night before, during dinner with her parents, he'd talked briefly about the space Rebecca had situated him in at the hospital, but he hadn't said much about the project he was working on there. And when he'd talked about it the other day right here in the diner, Bubba's arrival had interrupted.

"Reviewing five years' worth of research." He got up and went into the kitchen and returned a moment later with one of her sticky cinnamon rolls on a plate. He sat back down and cut the oversize roll in half before picking it up. "They're still hot." He took a bite and blew out a breath. "Really hot," he said, chewing fast.

She poured him a glass of water, slid it in front of him and went back to filling saltshakers.

"What's the research about?"

"I could tell you." His set down the roll and gulped down half the glass of water. "But then I'd have to kill you."

She rolled her eyes. "Well, you've already said it's not a cure for the common cold, so I know it's not that.

Some newfangled weight-loss pill? The next advance in the little blue pill for men who can't—"

"No. And no. But if the research bears out, then it could be another step forward in treating infertility."

She capped the last saltshaker. "You think something's wrong with the research?"

"I didn't say that."

"Your expression did."

"It wasn't my research project. I have no idea what I'll find."

"Whose project was it?" She told herself she was prepared for him to say Gillian's name, but when he didn't, she still felt her shoulders relax.

"A guy named Harmon Wethers."

"Why isn't he handling it?"

His lips twisted. "He's got other things to take care of right now. Regardless, *my* boss—Charles—assigned it to me. I've got a lot less time than I would if the research project had been one of my own design. We're both in research, but Wethers's area of expertise was entirely separate from mine, and there's a lot of stuff to validate before I can even start writing the paper."

Tabby studied him for a moment. "You're really worried you won't finish in time." It wasn't a question. She could see it in his eyes.

"Pretty much."

"What happens if you don't?"

"CNJ loses a whole lot of money."

"It's a multimillion-dollar company."

"And they'd be losing millions." He frowned slightly. "I'd just as soon not lose my job over it."

"You've been Charles Jennings's golden boy since you identified that one cancer strand thing right out of college—" She had the clippings about it from the medical journals still tucked away in her dresser.

"I wouldn't say golden," Justin countered. "But he has invested a lot in me, and now it's time for me to keep delivering. If I succeed, there should be a good promotion in it."

"The vice president deal?" She shrugged one shoulder when he gave her a surprised look. "Erik mentioned it."

"Yeah. The vice president deal."

She leaned over, folding her arms on the counter. "You don't sound entirely thrilled."

"It's what I've worked toward since before I even finished college."

She tucked her tongue behind her teeth for a moment. But she still couldn't stop herself. "Is it what you still want, though?"

"Why wouldn't it be?"

She shrugged her shoulders and dropped it. She used to dream of him wanting to come back to Weaver to stay, but time and experience had finally killed those thoughts off for the fantasies they were. "If anybody can do it, I'm sure you can. Even if it means proving the results aren't what everyone expects, you'll finish in time to meet your deadline."

His eyes met hers, and he smiled faintly.

And for a moment, her heart stopped a little.

She didn't even realize that Sloan McCray had entered the restaurant until he cleared his throat.

"Morning," he said, setting his travel mug next to the cash register with a bit of a thunk.

Her cheeks felt hot, and she straightened, quickly

grabbing the coffee carafe to fill his mug. "Cinnamon roll this morning?"

"Now that I'm addicted to them, yes." The deputy nodded toward the nearly decimated one on Justin's plate. "That's how it starts," he said. "You think you can have just one. Run a few hundred miles to work off the calories. But you keep coming back for another. Pretty soon, you're missing work, selling your dog. Anything for another fix—"

"Please." Tabby pushed the pastry box into his hand. The deputy was in superb condition. Even before he'd married Abby Marcum, every female in town had either wanted to marry him or mother him. "You come in because you like the coffee. Pam Rasmussen told me half the time you're auctioning off your roll to the other guys in the office."

The deputy smiled slightly. "Our dispatcher does like to talk."

"Along with nearly every other person who lives in Weaver," Justin added drily.

Sloan's smile widened a little, and Tabby wanted to cringe at the speculation in his eyes as he looked from Justin back to her again.

"Well." Sloan dropped a few bills in the tip jar. "Hope you two enjoy your, ah, morning." Still smiling slightly, he ambled out of the restaurant.

"Well, *that's* great," she muttered when the door closed and the bell jingled.

"What's that?"

She propped her hands on her hips. "You didn't see that look he gave us?" She tossed up her hands at the blank response she got.

"What?" He popped the rest of his roll in his mouth.

"Nothing." At least the deputy wasn't the kind to gossip the way Pam Rasmussen was. She plunked the coffee carafe on the counter in front of him. "I've got to get started on the hash browns for Bubba." She escaped into the kitchen. "Don't choke on that roll!"

Justin smiled at the door swinging to and fro after her and swallowed down his roll. Then he filled a to-go cup with coffee, added a few bucks of his own to the tip jar and headed out, the weight of his messenger bag bumping against his hip.

Things were getting back to normal with Tabby.

The day was looking up already.

Every year, Weaver's community tree lighting was the town's official kickoff for the holiday season.

About fifty Christmas trees—fresh, unlike the one at the diner—were set up in the town park at the end of the block and strung with lights. A band was on hand to play Christmas music. There was an enormous pot-luck, with everyone who could bringing covered dishes to share. They were arranged by the tree-lighting committee on plastic-covered plywood planks propped on barrels. Kids chased each other around. Adults overate and gossiped. And when it was time for the tree lights to come on, everyone gasped a little, cheered a little and felt swept up in the holiday spirit.

At least that's how it always worked for Tabby.

She didn't bring a dish from her own kitchen, though.

Using a three-shelved rolling cart from the restaurant, she wheeled over several serving pans of barbecue that Bubba had prepared at Ruby's. Pulled pork. Brisket. Shredded chicken. She had it all, plus fat, yeasty rolls on which to pile it. There was enough food on her rolling cart to feed a small army, and that's the way she liked it.

Because there were those families around who came to the event who *couldn't* bring a dish to share.

It was up to places like Ruby's to make sure that no one went away hungry.

Pam Rasmussen—the gossipy dispatcher from the sheriff's office—had been chairperson of the tree lighting for more years than Tabby could count. Pam grabbed her in an enthusiastic choke hold the second she spotted her. "Merry Christmas!"

Tabby laughed as much as her limited breath allowed and worked some distance between them. "Everything's looking great as always, Pam."

The other woman beamed. "I've got a table reserved just for your food." She admired the pans on the cart. "Can I peek?"

"Knock yourself out. It's exactly what you asked for at the last committee meeting."

Pam peeled up the foil edge covering the topmost pan. "Smells heavenly. My husband loves Bubba's brisket." She tucked the foil back in place. Then she straightened and pulled down the hem of her brilliant red sweatshirt festooned with a glittery snowman on the front. "Okay." She was clearly back in chairperson mode. "Your table is closest to the pavilion." She waved toward the round structure situated in the middle of the park.

"You moved the food this year?"

"We'll try it. Everyone sets up their picnic chairs to face the band in the pavilion, so I'm hoping with more focus in that direction, we won't have any incidents of kids spiking the punch like we did last year. If I could get the committee to agree that serving punch in punch bowls is passé, we wouldn't have that problem."

"I like the punch bowls," Tabby admitted. "It's tradition."

Pam made a face. "So is spiking them with booze when nobody is looking," she said drily.

"It only happens later in the evening when most of the folks with children have already gone home."

Pam propped her hand on her hip. "Please tell me you're not packing a fifth of vodka somewhere under that red sweater you're wearing."

Tabby laughed and held up her palm. "On my honor," she assured Pam and wheeled her cart in the direction of the pavilion.

Residents were beginning to show up in the park. Most of the picnic tables had already been staked out. There weren't enough there to accommodate all the people who would attend, so they were prime real estate. Others brought chairs of their own and blankets to spread out on the grass that had begun browning over a month ago. Some—like the Clays and her folks—brought their own folding tables to use.

After she'd stored her cart out of the way behind the pavilion, she headed toward her family's collection of tables.

She gave a general wave to all and sat down on the blanket next to her sister-in-law, Leandra. "Where are the kids?"

"Evan's got them over on the playground." Leandra leaned back against her hands and stretched out her legs, knocking the toes of her boots together. "You decided yet what you're going to wear to the hospital fund-raiser next weekend?"

Tabby shook her head. She kept forgetting that her brother had purchased a table at the event. "Can't I just wear the usual?"

Leandra laughed slightly. "Blue jeans and boots? It's cocktail attire, sweetheart. That means a dress, typically. Or at least some sparkle on slacks that aren't made of denim."

Tabby made a face. "Do you have anything in your closet that I can borrow?"

Leandra laughed wryly. "I don't have anything in my closet for *me*. Izzy is whipping up a dress for me, though. Talk to your mom. Maybe she can do the same thing for you."

Except her mother had already admitted she'd be making a dress for Vivian Templeton's hush-hush party. Nevertheless, Tabby glanced around. "Is she even here yet?" It was obvious to her that her parents weren't. But the person she was really looking for was Justin. Who was also absent.

"I talked to your mom an hour ago. They should be pulling in any minute. I need an idea what to get her for Christmas, too."

Tabby laughed ruefully. "That is an infectious problem, girlfriend. I saw a blouse over at Classic Charms that looked nice, but when I went back to buy it, it was gone. Sydney told me that she sold out half their stock last weekend with all the people in town for the pool tournament."

"Good for business. Bad for us. And one more reason I'm glad I've already talked to Izzy." Leandra suddenly lifted her hand in a wave and pushed to her feet. "I see Squire and Gloria. Going to go give them a hand."

Tabby waved at them but stayed put because she

spotted her brother crossing the grass from the playground with his kids in tow. She greeted them with hugs. Katie and Lucas both flopped down on the blanket beside her and started begging for food. They were four and six and full of energy. Hannah sat, too, but was quieter.

"Hey, bugs." Tabby leaned close to the girl. "Did you have fun at Grandma Helen's for Thanksgiving?"

Hannah nodded.

"Look what I brought for you." Tabby pulled a coloring book out of her oversize purse. "All of the pictures are flowers, just like you like. And—" she reached in her purse again and pulled out a small box "—brand-new crayons."

Hannah's eyes lit with delight. She had a particular fondness for new crayons, loving the way they were all the same length and the tips were sharp. "Just for me?"

"Just for you, bugs."

Hannah reached out and gave one of her rare hugs. "Thank you."

"You're welcome."

"What about us?" Lucas and Katie hung over her back, and Tabby laughed and pulled out two more boxes of crayons.

"You guys, too. But I thought you were all anxious to get your food?"

They snatched their crayons and spread out on their stomachs, dumping everything out in a haphazard pile while they flipped open their coloring books.

"Hey." Evan tugged her hair as he threw himself down among them. "How's my favorite sister?"

She barely had time to respond, because it seemed as though everyone in town suddenly descended on the park all at once. Tabby got up to help her nieces and nephew get settled with their plates of food, and then she got busy helping Pam keep the tables—which were groaning under the weight of potluck dishes—somewhat organized. She passed out paper plates, helped fill plastic cups with punch and carried servings of cake and pie to the masses. And all the while, she kept her eye out for Justin.

But he never showed.

She hated the disappointment that sat like a lump in her gut. If she hadn't expected him at all, she would have enjoyed the event as much as she always did.

Still, she kept a smile pinned on her face at least until the bulk of the people had departed and the band had packed up its instruments. There were only a few diehard celebrators hanging around after that. Someone was playing a radio loudly, and when Tabby checked the dwindling contents of the last punch bowl, she caught her breath at the strong alcohol content. Once again, despite Pam moving the serving tables, someone had managed to spike the punch.

There were only adults left in the park, so she didn't dump out the bowl, but left it and moved on to loading up the cart from her restaurant with her empty trays. She had plenty of light to work by. The white lights strung on the Christmas trees were still lit. From now until New Year's Day, they'd automatically turn on at dusk and off at dawn. With the music coming from the radio and the sound of laughter from the diehards, it wasn't unpleasant work.

She even poured herself a half cup of the spiked punch and sat down on the raised platform of the pavilion to sip it.

* * *

And that's where Justin found her.

Sitting on the edge of pavilion stage, with her legs hanging down, swinging them back and forth.

He couldn't help but smile at the sight as he walked toward her. "Remember when Joey Rasmussen got caught behind the pavilion making out with—"

"Yvonne Musgraves?" Tabby tilted her head slightly, and her hair slid over her shoulder. He saw how the Christmas tree lights were reflected in her eyes when he stopped in front of her. "Lots of kids got caught making out behind the pavilion."

He sat down beside her and dumped the messenger bag with his laptop and the files he still needed to go through that night next to him on the stage. "You didn't get caught."

"Because I never made out with anyone behind the pavilion." Her voice was dry.

"Ever?"

She let out an exasperated laugh. "Don't sound so shocked. Just because the spot was a hotbed of passion with the various girls you and Joey would get back there doesn't mean every high school kid was doing the same thing."

"I only ever took Collette back there," he retorted, defending himself. "But I think Joey had a different girl every week."

"He did have variety. Whereas you simply took Collette there every chance you got."

Tabby swung her legs a few times while they fell silent. Bob Dylan was singing about "Knockin' on Heaven's Door" from someone's radio. Justin inhaled the spicy scent put off by the dozens of Douglas fir trees and wondered when the last time was that he'd just sat somewhere to *be*.

Then his stomach growled, butting in on his uncommon contentment. He wished he hadn't lost track of time while he'd been working. He'd missed all the food. There was nothing left on the picnic tables except a big old-fashioned punch bowl that was nearly empty.

"Why'd you break up with her, anyway?"

He dragged his thoughts away from his stomach. "Who? Collette? She dumped *me*. In favor of her brother's college roommate. You ought to remember that. You were there when it happened."

"Not Collette."

She was talking about Gillian, he realized.

And the last person he wanted to talk about was Gillian. She was also the last person he wanted to think about.

"She slept with someone else." He leaned forward and looked toward the bare tables set up adjacent to the pavilion. "Is the punch any good?"

In answer, she handed him her plastic cup. "Spiked."

"It's ten at night. Of course it's spiked." He took a healthy swig and nearly coughed as it burned all the way down. "That's a helluva lot heavier a dose of spiking than we used to pull when we were young."

"Speak for yourself on that *we*," she said. "I never pulled that particular stunt. You forgave her the last time she did it."

Trust Tabitha Taggart not to be diverted from the conversation. "More fool on me."

"You'll forgive her this time, too."

He sighed. In the seven years of their on-again, off-again relationship, Gillian had never come home with him to Weaver. His brother and parents had only met her one time when they'd come to Boston and toured his lab at CNJ. Her disinterest in the people who mattered to him had been only one of the problems between them.

In hindsight, now that he'd finally made the break, it was easy to see how futile it all had been.

"I don't have to forgive her," he said. "When I realized I didn't even care, I knew I was done."

Tabby made a soft little humming sound of disbelief.

He didn't want to debate the topic with Tabby. There was no point to it, because there was no way she could possibly understand the level of done that he'd reached with Gillian.

As far as he knew, Tabby had never been involved with anyone beyond a few dates. If he'd taken a leaf from her book, he'd have moved past Gillian after two dates and saved himself a helluva lot of chaos.

He finished off the contents of Tabby's plastic cup, then pushed off the stage and stood. "What kind of food did I miss out on?"

"The usual. Fried chicken. Three-bean casseroles. Seven-layer salad with peas and cheese. About twenty boxes of pepperoni pizza and more store-bought pies than Shop-World carries. Bubba's barbecue."

His ears perked. "Bubba's barbecue? Any left?" His stomach growled again, right on cue.

And loud enough for her to hear, because she made a face and rolled her eyes before standing also.

"It's only because you own the place that I'll open up Ruby's in order to raid Bubba's leftovers."

He grinned and dropped his arm over her shoulder, ignoring her quick little flinch. "Bubba will never know," he promised.

Chapter Seven

Bubba knew.

And he complained about it through the entire morning rush the next day.

Tabby didn't usually work on Saturdays. But she'd gone to the diner to take care of the books, which she did in one of the corner booths, because Ruby's diner had never possessed something as fancy as an actual office space.

She had a filing cabinet shoved into one corner of the kitchen, along with several narrow lockers that the crew could use to store their personal belongings. But an office? A space to house a computer, a desk or even the phone?

That hadn't been necessary in Ruby Leoni's day, and Tabby—who'd been managing the place longer than anyone else besides Ruby—hadn't found it necessary, either.

Even if it did take a table out of the rotation on a particularly busy Saturday morning.

"You leave setting the special to me," Bubba said, dropping a hand-scrawled sheet of paper on her table as he passed by with a loaded tray to deliver to a six top. "Can't do that when you're comin' in all hours of the night, eatin' it up."

"I think the customers will survive, Bubba." Her voice was mild. She was used to Bubba's occasional dramatic flare-ups. They'd been coming a little more frequently since he'd started cooking privately for Vivian Templeton, but Tabby blamed that on Vivian's regular chef, Montrose. According to Hayley, Montrose was pretty much a monstrosity in the personality department. The chef had been with Hayley's grandmother back in Pennsylvania, and to say he had a highfalutin attitude was putting it mildly. "Instead of the special, they'll order off the menu. No harm in that."

"Harm in not having any pulled pork when folks come wanting it," he muttered after he'd delivered his tray and was heading back to the kitchen.

"Then put it on the menu."

If the temperature hadn't taken a nosedive overnight, she'd have just worked out back, where they had a grassy, treed area with a picnic table to use during breaks. But the weather was hovering below freezing, and she wasn't a glutton for punishment. She also could have worked at home, but the sight of Justin's truck parked outside had made her too antsy to stay there.

She wrote out the last of the paychecks for the month as well as the handful of bills and logged everything into the laptop computer sitting open on the table in front of her. She'd take the checks out to the Rocking C for Erik to sign sometime that weekend if he didn't come into town before then. She looked over Bubba's scrawled list of supplies and ingredients and put together an order for the coming week. Some things—

like the strawberry jam, the dairy and the eggs—she sourced locally. Other staples—flour, sugar and the like—she got from distributors out of Casper or Cheyenne, occasionally even Denver, depending on where she could get the best deals.

For a small-town diner, the quantity of food they went through was almost shocking. But she'd long ago realized that—whatever else might be going on in the world—people still found their way to Ruby's for a cup of joe and a bite to eat.

And thank goodness for it, or she wasn't sure what she'd be doing with her life. Painting was something she enjoyed. But she'd realized a long time ago that it didn't feed her soul the way running Ruby's did.

She smiled to herself. She fed others to feed herself.

"What're you sitting there grinning about?" Justin slid into the bench opposite her.

She looked at him over the screen of the laptop and only smiled a little wider. She couldn't help it.

It was Saturday. Her bookkeeping was done, and it felt like all was right with the world. "Snow," she answered him. "Weatherman's calling for it by tonight."

He shook his head. "I talked to my uncle Matt this morning. He said it wasn't coming yet. And you know his nose for snow."

She wasn't going to let him rain on her parade. "Well, maybe the famous Matthew Clay nose will be wrong for once. It could happen."

"Anything *could* happen," he allowed. "But it won't snow yet. Not today."

She closed the laptop and tucked the checks to be signed into a folder. "Usually by the beginning of December we've had at least *one* snow. Even if it doesn't stick. But not this year. Did you come in for breakfast?"

"What else?"

She smiled through the sting. It was silliness in the extreme to entertain the idea he might have come to see *her*. Particularly when he was staying two doors away from her. "As long as you're not wanting pulled pork barbecue for breakfast, you're in the right place." She slid out of the booth. "What'll it be?"

"Pancakes and sausage."

"Turkey or regular?"

He looked surprised. "You serve turkey sausage now?"

"Gotta change with the times," she drawled. "We even have a quinoa salad and cucumber water. The mayor's wife is partial to both. So what'll it be?"

"Regular."

"Coming up." She went over to the counter to give Bubba the order. The other waitresses were all busy, so she started a fresh pot of coffee in the brewer and carried the carafe back to fill Justin's mug.

He'd flipped open her folder of checks and was fanning through them. "They're not signed."

"Erik signs them."

She moved to the next table, holding up the carafe. "Refills for you?" Both young men—she was pretty sure they worked out at Cee-Vid—pushed their empty mugs toward her. She filled them and continued around the diner, greeting and filling until the carafe was empty and she moved the freshly full one onto a warmer and started another pot. She'd barely finished that when the delivery truck came with a package. She signed for it and peeked inside, recognizing the custom-made storybook she'd ordered for Hannah for Christmas, and stored it in her locker in the kitchen. Then she delivered Justin's pancakes to him, along with a little pitcher of warm maple syrup.

"Anything else?"

"Yeah." He stuck the checks back in the folder and gestured at the empty bench across from him. "Sit. I thought you didn't work on Saturdays."

She sat. "This isn't work."

He snorted softly. "Most people would disagree. Want a pancake?" He lifted the edge of the one on top of his stack.

"Nope."

He let the edge down and dumped the entire pitcher of syrup on top. "Why don't you sign the checks?"

"Because I'm not on the bank account. No reason to be." Neither was he, but only because he hadn't been around to add his name to the account when Erik had changed banks several years ago.

"You should be." He took a mammoth-size bite of syrup-drenched pancake and gestured slightly with his fork. "You take care of everything else around here. What happens if Erik's not around to sign a check and you need money for something?"

She lifted her eyebrows. "I've got petty cash. It's a system that's been working for a lot of years. Why are you suddenly so interested?"

He shrugged and attacked his pancakes again with the enthusiasm of a man who hadn't eaten in days, much less twelve hours ago in this very restaurant. "I've always been interested."

She could have argued the point but couldn't imagine to what purpose. Interested or not in the management of the place, he was still one of the owners. "Did you get your homework done last night?" Over Bubba's purloined pulled pork, he'd told her about the work he still needed to get through.

He nodded and shoveled more pancake into his mouth.

"You're gonna choke," she said drily and got up again to make another round with the coffee. Hayley and her new husband, Seth, came in before she was finished, and she gestured toward a booth that had just been cleared. "Be right with you two."

The couple smiled and crossed toward the booth, stopping to say a few hellos on the way.

Tabby headed back toward Justin when the door jingled again, and she looked toward it, a greeting already on her lips.

She'd only ever seen Gillian Jennings in a photograph. A snapshot that Justin had pulled out of his wallet ages ago when he had started dating the woman in college.

But Tabby recognized her now. From the top of her gleaming light blond hair to the toes of her expensive, ridiculously high-heeled pumps.

Feeling something go cold inside her, she approached the newcomer, anyway. "Can I help you with something?"

The woman smiled, seeming friendly enough. "Directions, I'm hoping. All the cars on the street are parked in front of this place."

"It's a busy morning." Tabby wondered how long it would be before Justin would look up from his pancakes to see his erstwhile lover standing fifteen feet away. "Directions where?"

Gillian pulled a piece of paper from the pocket of the light brown leather jacket that fit her svelte figure like a glove and read off the address of Tabby's triplex. "I'm looking for my fiancé," she added with a smile.

Tabby went a lot colder. "Oh," she inquired with amazing mildness. "What's his name?"

Gillian tucked away the paper again. "Justin. Justin Clay. He always said Weaver was a small town, but I never imagined just how small. Do you know him?"

Tabby smiled humorlessly and held out her hand toward the corner booth. "As a matter of fact, I do. Obviously not as well as I thought, though." She raised her voice. "Justin? Somebody here to see you."

He looked up, his expression instantly thunderstruck.

Tabby didn't wait around to see any more.

While Gillian gave a little shriek of delighted surprise and clattered on her high heels toward him, Tabby turned on her heel and went through to the kitchen and straight on out the rear door.

Justin looked from the swinging kitchen door to Gillian's face and didn't manage to act fast enough to avoid the arms she threw around his neck as she sat down on the bench seat beside him.

He wanted to curse.

Instead, he looked into Gillian's deceitful green eyes and pulled on her arms. "What are you doing here?"

She pouted a little but let go of the neck lock. "You've always wanted me to come with you to Weaver." She looked at his nearly empty plate and gave a shudder of horror. "Pancakes? Honey, all those carbs—"

"We broke up," he interrupted her. "Remember?"

She waved her hand dismissively. "I know you didn't

really mean it." She snuggled close to his side. "That's what passionate couples like us do. We break up. We make up."

He would have scooted farther away if he weren't already wedged in the corner of the booth thanks to the way she'd launched herself at him. "Not this time." Since he couldn't move one direction, he moved the other, shoving her along to the edge of the booth. "Get up."

She didn't have any choice but to scramble somewhat inelegantly to her feet. It was either that or get pushed off onto the butt of her expensive suede pants. "Justin, honey, don't be difficult now. You had to know I'd come. That's what you wanted, isn't it? For me to run after you for once?"

As busy as Ruby's was, her words were still plainly audible to those around them, and Justin felt an urge to wrap his hands around her throat to stop them. Since he wasn't inclined to be convicted of strangling a lying woman, he grabbed her arm instead and pulled her toward the front door. "Bubba," he yelled toward the kitchen, "put Tabby's laptop and files away for her."

Then he marched Gillian out the front door and onto the sidewalk. "You know why I'm not working in Boston," he said through his teeth. "Because you weren't giving me an hour's rest getting through Harmon's project!"

She had to know he was livid, but that had never stopped Gillian. She walked her fingertips up his chest, tilting her head back so her thick blond hair streamed down to the small of her back and she could look coyly at him through her long lashes. "You used to like my little visits to your lab," she said. "Remember?"

He grabbed her hand and deliberately set it away from him. "That look might have worked on me once, but it's lost its appeal. I damn sure didn't come here so you could chase after me!" He wanted to groan when he noticed the couple just rounding the corner on the sidewalk as they headed toward Ruby's. Pam and Rob Rasmussen.

"Justin!" Pam waved merrily at him as she and her husband reached the café's glass door. "I heard you were still in town. We missed you last night at the tree lighting." Her inquisitive gaze lingered on Gillian. "How have you been?"

"Fine, Pam." He wished she'd just go inside. But naturally, that would be too simple for the hell his life had suddenly become.

"I'm Pam Rasmussen." She stuck out her hand toward Gillian. "Justin and I go way back. And you're…" She raised her brows, waiting.

"Gillian Jennings," Justin said at the same time Gillian did.

Only Gillian went even further. She laughed lightly, as if such a thing happened all the time, and bumped her gilded head against Justin's sleeve. "Justin's fiancée," she added.

Pam's jaw dropped, and Justin grabbed Gillian's arm again, tightening his hand warningly.

"Not my fiancée," he said to Pam. But he knew the damage was already done. No matter what he said to her, she'd have him walking down the aisle with Gillian by the time she finished spreading the latest news. "Excuse us," he said before pulling Gillian farther down the street. He didn't stop until he reached the borrowed pickup truck and pulled open the door. "Get in."

She gave the ancient truck a wary look but climbed up gingerly onto the seat.

All the annoyance he felt came out in the slam of the truck door when he shut it.

Then he rounded the truck, momentarily distracted by the sight of a Rolls-Royce driving down the middle of the street before he got behind the wheel. He didn't start the engine. "Are you insane?"

She gave a huffy sniff. "There's no need to be mean."

"And there's damn sure no need for you to be here in Weaver. Much less announcing you're my fiancée!" God only knew what his folks would think when they heard the gossip.

And they would.

To think otherwise would be as insane as Gillian still thinking they had any sort of future together.

And then there was Tabby.

He wasn't going to forget the look on her face in a lifetime of Saturday pancakes, and that was a certainty.

"You know we never agreed on getting married even when we were together." His voice was flat.

"That's just because we were both so wrapped up in our careers. In the success of CNJ. We're meant to be together. You're going to be Daddy's successor. Everyone knows it. We're the perfect couple!"

He was getting a pain in his head. He felt as if she was actually going to cause him a nosebleed. "You've got to be kidding me. What was so perfect that it landed you in bed with another guy? *Again?*"

"I told you that was a mistake. I told you I wanted to start fresh. That I needed a…a real sign from you that you wanted to be with me."

She was exhausting. She might be brilliant when it

came to developing CNJ's line of consumer products, but when it came to the usual logic of surviving every day with other human beings—much less the personal relationships with them—she completely missed the boat. Her reasoning defied explanation.

That fact might have charmed him when they'd been college students, but it had entirely lost its luster.

"What I told you over a *year* ago," he said bluntly, "was that I needed a sign from you that you were done playing games. Which is all you've done in the time since. I told you six months ago we were through. Over. Done. Not together. Not ever going to be together again. And I've repeated it just about every damn week since. How much clearer do I have to be?"

She put on her pouty face again. "But my coming here *is* a sign, honey. I even brought you a surprise."

Beyond the unwelcome surprise of her presence? "I don't want surprises, Gillian."

"You'll want this one." She pushed open the truck door and trotted down the sidewalk, disappearing around the corner.

It would be too much to hope that she wouldn't return. And if he drove away, she'd just come after him again. He knew from experience that she could be relentless when she set her mind to something.

She reappeared around the corner, her blond hair rippling around her shoulders and the unidentifiable bundle she held in her arms.

Then she reached his truck and pulled open the door.

"See?" She smiled brilliantly, ever confident in her own appeal and manipulations as she set the bundle on the truck seat beside him. "Here's proof."

The bundle wriggled, looking up at him with big

brown eyes and a wagging tail. Then the puppy woofed and hopped onto Justin's lap.

He automatically caught the small beagle pup and moved his hand away from the sharp little teeth. "My hand's not a chew toy, little girl," he murmured and looked again at Gillian.

"I knew you couldn't resist a puppy. You've talked about wanting a dog for years," she said. "That's why he's the perfect peacemaking gift." She ran her hands down her slender hips. "We'll raise him and he'll be the perfect dog when we start our family."

Horror engulfed him. "You didn't cook all this up because you're pregnant, did you?"

She looked insulted. "Do I look fat and pregnant to you?"

She looked the same as always. Very thin. Very blonde. Impressively spoiled and inherently selfish.

There was no way any baby she carried could be his. The last time they'd slept together was more than six months ago. She'd have to be showing a decent-size baby bump by now if she were going to claim it was his.

That didn't mean there were no other possible sources of paternity. With Gillian, there were probably more than a few.

But no matter how much Charles Jennings had spoiled his daughter, he wouldn't take kindly to the idea of her having a baby outside of marriage. So at least if she were pregnant, it would explain her unexpected appearance in Weaver. She'd need a husband and right quick.

"Yes or no, Gillian. Are you pregnant?"

She huffed. "No, I am not pregnant."

The puppy squirmed in his lap and started chewing on the ridged steering wheel.

Justin scooped his hand beneath the warm fat belly and held the puppy out to her. "Take the pup—who is a *she*—back to wherever you got her and go home, Gillian."

"But—"

"Take. The. Dog."

She made a face and took the puppy, who whined and scratched her paws against Gillian's leather jacket. "It's not going to be that easy to get rid of me, Justin," she warned, though she had the good sense to back out of the way when he reached across the cab of the truck and yanked the door closed. "I'm not giving up on us!"

He cranked the engine and drove off. When he glanced in his rearview mirror, he saw her standing in the belch of smoke the truck had let out.

He hoped it would be the last he saw of her.

When he got to the triplex, there was no sign of Tabby. He even checked with Mrs. Wachowski but the old woman just shook her white-haired head.

He drove back through town hoping to spot Tabby but steered clear of the restaurant on the off chance that Gillian was still hanging around like an infection. When he reached Shop-World at the other end of town without spotting Tabby, though, he admitted the futility of the exercise. Particularly when he didn't even know whether she drove the same car she used to.

He stopped in a parking lot next to a park that hadn't existed a year ago and pulled out his cell phone. The signal strength was a little better there than it was at the triplex.

He called Tabby's folks' number, but all he got was

the sound of her dad's voice on the answering machine. He knew she had friends, but the notion of calling all over town trying to hunt her down had no appeal, since it would just add fuel to the perpetually turning gossip wheel.

Instead, he dialed Charles at his home and asked the man to rein in his daughter before Justin lost his temper entirely. It was obvious that Charles had no idea what Gillian had done, and the older man assured Justin he'd take care of the matter.

He'd better. Right now, Charles needed Justin to finish the infertility project more than he needed his spoiled little girl to get back the toy she wanted to toss around.

Then, out of ideas, he drove back through town to the hospital.

He couldn't do anything about Tabby until he found her. But at least he could do what he was in town in the first place to do.

Work.

He just wished it held as much satisfaction as it used to.

Chapter Eight

"Tabby, dear." Mrs. Wachowski's voice came through the front door, accompanied by knocking. "Are you home?"

Sighing, Tabby threw off the blanket she'd been huddling beneath since she'd left her brother's vet practice, where she'd gone after walking out of Ruby's that morning, and padded to the front door. She unlocked it and peeked around the edge at her elderly neighbor.

From the scarf tied over her white hair to the low-heeled black pumps she wore on her feet, the short, round woman was clearly dressed for an outing. "You look nice, Mrs. Wachowski. Bingo night in Braden with Mr. Rowe again?"

The woman's head bobbed. "I thought young Justin would be here by now, and I just don't know what to do with her."

Tabby's jaw tightened. "Do with who?"

Mrs. Wachowski shifted, and Tabby spotted the leash she was holding. "The puppy, of course. That pretty fiancée of his left the puppy with me around three because he wasn't home when she came by, but it's six now and I thought he'd certainly be back."

The knot in the pit of her stomach tightened, but she opened the door wider. Sure enough, there was a small brown-and-white puppy at the end of the leash. A puppy who was trying to attack the brick edging of the flower bed lining the front of the triplex.

If Justin wasn't with his *fiancée*, he was probably working. She crouched down and clapped her hands together, drawing the puppy's attention. "Did she say anything else?" Like when the wedding would be? The thought was bitter.

"His fiancée?" Mrs. Wachowski adjusted her scarf slightly and checked her wristwatch. She'd been a stickler for punctuality when she taught high school history and hadn't changed since then. "I was surprised to hear he was engaged, of course. He never mentioned it, even when he was helping me this morning with my furnace."

Justin hadn't mentioned anything to Tabby about helping Mrs. Wachowski, either. Seemed not mentioning things had become his new normal. "What's wrong with your furnace?" The puppy sniffed her way around Mrs. Wachowski's shoes, making her way toward Tabby's fingers.

"Nothing now. The pilot light was out, but he got it going again."

"That's good."

"So what do you think I should do about the puppy?" Mrs. Wachowski looked concerned. "If I leave her alone in my unit, I'm afraid she'll have an accident or two. She's not house-trained in the least. And she wants to chew on everything."

"She's a puppy," Tabby murmured. "Puppies chew."

As evidenced by the way the dog pounced on her fingers. "What's her name?"

"His fiancée never said, actually." Mrs. Wachowski carefully lifted one foot then her other out from the loop in the leash the dog had made around her. "I did think that was odd, but—" She made a worried sound. "There's Mr. Rowe now, ready to drive us to bingo. I don't suppose I could impose on you to—"

"I'll watch the puppy," Tabby said wearily. She scooped up the dog and stood. "Did she—" she couldn't bring herself to say Gillian's name "—leave food or anything else for the dog?"

Mrs. Wachowski handed over the leather leash handle. "Not a single thing. I fed the little beastie some bread that I crumbled up with chicken stock. I didn't know what else to do."

"That's more than a lot would do," Tabby assured her. "Go and enjoy your bingo, Mrs. Wachowski. The puppy will be fine until Justin gets back."

The woman was clearly relieved. "You're such a sweet girl, Tabby."

The puppy switched her attention to Tabby's face, enthusiastically swiping her tongue over every part she could reach. "That's me," Tabby muttered as she watched Mrs. Wachowski scurry to the curb and Mr. Rowe in his waiting car. "Sweet, foolish Tabby."

She watched them drive around the corner and then set the dog on the brown grass. "Don't suppose you know how to potty on command, do you?"

The puppy scampered toward the sidewalk, squatted and peed on the cement.

"Well. It's better than my living room rug." She

tugged gently on the leash. "Come, little beastie. Let's go inside."

Which were words the dog seemed to recognize, because she bounded up the porch step and darted inside, yanking the leash handle right out of Tabby's relaxed grip. A second later, she heard a crash and a yelp, and she vaulted after the pup.

Inside, the lamp that usually sat on Tabby's narrow entryway table was lying on its side on the floor. The white shade was split, but the lightbulb was still intact. "No harm." Tabby set the lamp where it belonged and rubbed the puppy's head.

It wasn't the dog's fault her owner was engaged to an idiot male who didn't know better than to trust a faithless woman.

"Come on." She unclipped the leash from the puppy's too-large blue collar, picked her up and returned to the protective cocoon she'd made for herself on the couch.

The dog immediately burrowed into Tabby's fluffy blanket and tucked her wet nose against Tabby's neck.

She stroked the warm, smooth coat. "I should get myself one of you," she said on a sigh. "My brother takes care of beasties like you. From tiny puppies all the way up to huge horses and most everything in between. If I tell him I want a dog, he'll find one of his many strays and be on my doorstep in two shakes." She looked into the dog's inquisitive brown eyes. "He wanted me to take a cat last year. But I'm afraid of turning into the spinster cat lady." She rested her cheek on the top of the dog's head.

The phone sitting on her end table rang, and she reached blindly to pick it up. "This is your friendly neighborhood dog-sitting service," she said robotically. "Please leave your message after the tone."

"Dog sitting, huh?" Sam Dawson's voice held laughter.

"Hey, Sam." Tabby grabbed the television remote and muted the black-and-white movie she'd been watching. "Diner's closed tomorrow if you're needing more cinnamon rolls."

"Not this time. I wanted to see if you were interested in going to Colbys tonight. Hayley and I are going. Girls' night."

"Why isn't Hayley home romancing her new handsome husband?"

"He's working security out at Cee-Vid tonight."

Covering for another one of the security guards, Tabby guessed, since Seth usually worked days. "I'd go, but I'm puppy sitting," she said, and the sittee in question gave a little woof and started chewing on the point of Tabby's chin. She winced and covered the pooch's muzzle. "No biting."

"If you hadn't just said you were puppy sitting, I'd wonder what was going on over there," Sam said on a chuckle. "You've really got a puppy there?"

"Well, I don't have a man," Tabby returned darkly.

"You would if you ever said yes to the guys who ask you out."

"Is this a lecture on my love life or an invitation to girls' night?"

"You don't have a love life."

"Don't remind me." Tabby redirected the puppy's interest away from chewing on her face again. "*No biting.* And I don't recall you being in the company of any eligible males lately."

"I work with a few dozen every day."

"Socially."

"Ah, well, that's a different story. Sure you don't want to come? Get one of your neighbors to watch the pooch?"

It would serve Justin right if she closed Beastie in his apartment, unsupervised. Let the little girl go crazy, chewing and knocking things over. Maybe give him a nice puddle to slip in when he got home.

"He deserves it, but you don't," she murmured to the dog.

"Talking Greek there, girlfriend."

Tabby tucked the phone against her shoulder and leaned over to set the puppy on the floor. "Sorry, Sam. I would come if I could. A girls' night sounds like just the ticket right now, but I can't."

"This have anything to do with your hunky renter's marital plans?"

Ugh. "Where'd you hear?"

Sam snorted softly. "In the line at Shop-World while I was buying kale and green tea. In the salon when I stopped in to get my hair trimmed. At the Gas 'n' Go when I was filling up. Plus, Hayley and Seth were at the diner this morning. Shall I go on?"

Tabby closed her eyes. "That's what this sudden girls' night is about?" Yes, she was friends with Sam, but they'd only met up the way she was suggesting a few times before.

"Nope. Seth's honestly working. I haven't had sex in six months, and I'm looking for a likely prospect at Colbys. But a girl always needs her wingmen."

Despite herself, Tabby chuckled. It was hard not to,

when it came to Sam. "Fine. But I still have a puppy here who shouldn't be left to her own devices."

"Bring her along, then," Sam said. "Put her in a purse and carry her on your arm like some rich girl from Beverly Hills."

"I don't have a dog-friendly purse," Tabby said drily. But she did have a veterinarian brother. "Fine." She pushed out of her blanket cocoon again and stood. "What time will you be there?"

"Sevenish."

Allowing her enough time to shower, dress and drop off Beastie at Evan's. "All right. But if I end up not showing, don't worry about me. It just means my brother couldn't watch the dog after all."

"Fair enough." Sam rang off, and Tabby looked down at the puppy. She'd sprawled beneath the glass-topped coffee table and was trying to wrap her jaws around one of the wooden legs.

"Sure," Tabby said, tugging the dog free and propping her against her shoulder. "Leave scars. It's only fitting."

The puppy shivered with delight and slathered Tabby's neck with her tongue.

An hour later, freshly showered and dressed in the most presentable pair of jeans she possessed and a thick oat-colored knit turtleneck, she left her house with Beastie on the leash and headed toward her 1979 Buick parked in the triple-wide driveway.

She had just spread a towel on the backseat for Beastie to sit on when Justin's truck pulled up.

She wanted to ignore him. To settle Beastie on the backseat, get in her car and drive away.

But Beastie was *his* dog.

His and Gillian's.

So she crossed her arms and leaned back against the open door and waited.

She didn't have to wait long. The truck's headlights had barely gone out before he climbed out and his long stride carried him rapidly across the lawn.

"That's *your* car?"

She stiffened. "You're not exactly driving the newest model off the production floor." And she happened to know that he didn't even own a vehicle in Boston. "I bought it from Mrs. Wachowski when she had to give up driving. It was her husband's."

He stopped a foot away. "I only meant—" He shook his head, looking impatient. "Where have you been all day?"

"I'm sorry. I wasn't aware that I had to account to you for my personal time. I guess I missed that clause in my employment contract at Ruby's."

"Dammit, Tab—"

"Here." She pushed Beastie into his arms.

"What the hell?"

"Don't drop her. She's just a baby."

"I know what she is!"

The puppy whined, and Tabby snatched her back, cuddling her against her chin. "If you're going to yell, then maybe I should wait until Gillian gets here!"

He shoved his fingers through his hair, and even though the three porch lights on the front of the triplex weren't very bright, she could see he'd left the thick, dark blond strands standing on end. "Gillian was here," he said, sounding like he was talking through his teeth.

"Obviously." Tabby stroked the puppy's back. "She

dumped off your puppy on Mrs. Wachowski. So where is she?"

"Mrs. Wachowski?"

Tabby very nearly stomped her boot. "Gillian!"

The puppy woofed shrilly and Tabby patted her shaking back. "Sorry, Beastie."

"Beastie?"

"Well, your *fiancée* didn't see fit to tell Mrs. Wachowski what this little girl's name was, much less leave any food or toys. So what is her name?"

"I have no idea," he shouted.

Tabby cuddled the puppy. "I warned you about yelling." She pushed the car door closed and headed toward her front door.

Justin grabbed her elbow from behind. "Not so fast."

She yanked free. "Don't touch me!" Beastie whined again, and she tucked her against her other shoulder, patting her again to calm her. "All the years I've known you, I've *never* thought you were a liar, Justin Clay. But to lie about Gillian? What good did that do you? Is your ego so monumental that you needed your childhood friend to swallow your story, hook, line and sinker? What was the point, when you *had* to know I'd learn the truth sooner or later? For God's sake. Why couldn't you have just admitted you were marrying her?"

"I am *not* marrying Gillian." He was talking through his teeth again. "I did not lie about her. I did not *lie* about one damn thing. You're more than a childhood friend. You're my best friend. And she was supposed to take that bloody puppy with her this morning when I told her to leave me the hell alone."

Tabby gave a disbelieving sniff. "The entire town has heard about your engagement."

"Yeah, and the Weaver grapevine proves itself to be as inaccurate as it always is. Something I spent an hour reminding my *mother* about when she called me on the carpet for not telling her the supposed news."

"If you told Gillian to leave, what was she doing coming here and leaving Beastie with Mrs. Wachowski?"

He threw his arms out to his sides. "It'd take more brilliance than I possess to ever explain why Gillian does what she does!" He let his arms drop. "She's bat-crap crazy. You going to believe the word of a crazy person or the guy you've known your whole damn life? I told you Gillian and I were through."

Tabby set Beastie on the ground between them, and the puppy immediately squatted, leaving another puddle on the cement driveway. Then she stood, looking up at them and wagging her curving tail so enthusiastically her butt swayed back and forth, too.

"And I warned you that you weren't," Tabby said and handed him the leash.

Then she got in the ancient car, started up the engine and drove away.

She'd never felt more in need of a girls' night.

"He really said she was bat-crap crazy?" Sam Dawson propped her elbow on the round high-top table they were occupying at Colbys and leaned closer.

Tabby had already gone through the story once. "The point is—" she drained her wineglass and reached for the bottle sitting between her and Sam and Hayley "—Gillian left him with a *dog*. They're not through. They'll never be through."

Hayley's eyes were compassionate. She was the town

psychologist, so Tabby figured that expression was simply ingrained. "And that is upsetting to you because…"

"Because he's my friend," Tabby muttered. "She's yanked him around on the 'Gillian chain—'" she air quoted the term with her fingers "—for years now."

"But if she is his choice, then as his *friend*, shouldn't you be happy for him?"

Tabby glared at Sam. "Whose side are you on?"

Sam grinned and lifted her hands peaceably. "Just playing devil's advocate here."

"Well, don't." Tabby took another sip of wine. Okay, perhaps more than a sip. Her adrenaline was pumping so strongly, she felt as though she was going to vibrate off the bar stool. "He's got terrible taste in women. He always has."

"Sure, 'cause those women aren't you," Sam returned.

Tabby's lips parted. "I don't know what you mean," she lied. But it was a half beat too late, and she saw the look Sam and Hayley exchanged.

She exhaled noisily. "You have a service weapon, Sam. Just shoot me."

"Ha-ha." Sam rolled her eyes. "What you need—" she leaned forward again "—is a man. Someone to get horizontal with and make you forget the unattainable one."

Hayley tsked. "Sam. Honestly."

"What? She's single and well past the age of consent. So—" Sam gestured at the bar, where a half dozen men in jeans and boots were hanging out, drinking beer and watching the television hanging on the wall at the end of the glossy wooden bar top "—take a gander."

"I've known every one of them since I was in diapers," Tabby objected. "I couldn't have a romantic thought about them if I had *three* bottles of wine." She poured more into her glass and frowned a little when she got only a few drops.

"What about one you haven't known all your life?" Sam nudged her boot under the table when the front door of Colbys opened and two tall men—both wearing green hospital scrubs beneath their coats—walked in. "That's Scott Brown with Wyatt Mead. He just started working at the hospital last year. And he comes from Braden."

"How do you know that?"

"Because I had to write Mr. Brown a speeding ticket this summer. He tried talking his way out of it by saying how he was new here and stuff."

Hayley chuckled and shook her head. "I guess that's *one* way of eliciting information."

"Have you known *him* all of your life?" Sam's voice was challenging.

The thought of going out with someone held no appeal. But she couldn't spend her days pining after Justin, either. She'd never move out of the perpetual friend category with him. He'd made that abundantly clear.

But Justin was going to be in Weaver until January. She couldn't escape that fact. So if she didn't want to spend her spare time cleaning kennel cages at her brother's practice to avoid running into him at the triplex, or cocooned in her blankets, or drowning herself in a bottle of wine, she'd better come up with an alternative.

Buoyed by adrenaline and wine and hurt she had no business feeling, anyway, she slapped her hand lightly on the top of their table. "You're right," she told Sam, and hopped off the high bar stool.

Scott and Wyatt had reached the bar and were waiting to give their orders to Merilee, who was bartending that night. Tabby stopped next to them. "Hey, Wyatt." She didn't give herself a chance to stop and get all girlie and stupid. "How're you doing? Haven't seen you in Ruby's in a few weeks." The tall, lanky nurse usually stopped by for coffee several times a week.

Wyatt looked chagrined. "Yeah, I've been—"

"Getting his morning coffee fix from his new squeeze," his companion said easily and stuck out his hand toward Tabby. "I'm Scott."

She set her hand in his. He had a good grip. "Tabby."

"Buy you a drink, Tabby?"

Despite her intention of introducing herself to *him*, Tabby was a little nonplussed at the way the tables had turned so quickly.

So easily.

"Um…sure. Red wine. Jane's got a nice house red." Scott had a nice smile, she decided while he ordered drinks. Not too friendly. Not too wicked. And his eyes were a very ordinary brown. Not an otherworldly shade of purplish blue.

She slid onto the empty bar stool between the two men when Scott pulled it out for her. "So are you an RN like Wyatt?"

Scott shook his head. "I work in the lab."

"He usually works nights," Wyatt told her. He pulled a folded clip of cash out of his pocket and paid Merilee when she delivered their drinks. "Next round's on you, bud," he told Scott.

"I took a shift today for one of the guys on days," Scott said. "Now I'm particularly glad I did." He smiled

at her and tapped the edge of his wineglass—also red—
against the edge of hers.

Tabby smiled and sipped her wine.

He worked in the lab. *Where Justin is temporarily
working.* She gave the voice in her head a mental shove.

"So you own Ruby's?"

She shook her head, letting out a rueful laugh. "I
only manage it." *For Justin.*

She shoved harder.

"Haven't made it over there," Scott said. "But everyone around the hospital says it's the best place for
breakfast."

"I like to think so. We have a great crew working
there." She looked at Wyatt. "But I guess our coffee is
taking second place to someone else's. Who is she?"

Wyatt flushed a little. "She's new in town. Works
out at Cee-Vid designing computer games."

"Well, I think that's great," she said sincerely. Wyatt
was a genuinely nice guy. He deserved to find a genuinely nice girl. "I hope it works out for you."

"She'll be with me at the hospital fund-raiser next
weekend," he said. "You're going to be there, right?"

She'd forgotten about the fund-raiser again. "I am."
She looked at Scott. "My brother has the vet practice
in town. He bought a table and needs people to fill the
chairs so it won't be empty. What about you?"

"Dr. Clay wants to trot out the lab rats at the event,"
he said humorously. "So, yeah. I'll be there."

"You two should go together," Wyatt suggested,
looking enthusiastic. "And double with me and Kristen."

Scott lifted his eyebrows. "What d'ya say? You won't

have to sit at your brother's table *all* evening long, will you?"

Tabby hesitated. She glanced over her shoulder at Sam and Hayley. Sam was giving her a none-too-subtle thumbs-up. But it was the sight of Justin walking through the front door of Colbys that made the decision for her.

She looked back at Scott.

"I think it sounds perfect," she said. "I'd love to go with you to the fund-raiser."

Chapter Nine

"Hey, Justin. Heard congratulations are in order."
Sally Gunderson smiled up from the table where she sat
outside the large white tent that had been set up behind
the hospital to house the fund-raiser. He remembered
her easily from high school, pretty much because she
hadn't changed a lick. "Here are your drink tickets."
She handed over two red tickets that she peeled off a
big roll. "Is your fiancée with you?"

After a week of explaining to everyone who mentioned it that he was *not* engaged, Justin was heartily
sick of it. "No." He tucked the tickets in the pocket of
the suit coat he'd borrowed from Jake. JD's husband
was one of the few guys in town to actually own a suit
that wasn't twenty years old. Justin's dad had plenty,
but he'd have looked like a kid playing dress-up if he'd
tried to wear one of Tristan's jackets. Justin was tall. But
he wasn't a freaking Paul Bunyan the way his dad was.

He focused on Sally. There were several racks standing behind her tables that were loaded down with coats.
"I'm supposed to sit at one of the tables the Double-C
purchased. Are they marked, or what?"

"Yup." She handed over a small tented place card. "Double-C" had been printed on one side and a number on the other. "Number four," she said, needlessly, since he could read well enough. "You're the last one to get here." She waved her hand over the table where only a few place cards remained. "But you're still here in plenty of time for dinner. They haven't even finished the speeches yet."

"Thanks." He wanted to attend the fund-raiser the way he wanted to have a hole drilled in his head. He knew that his dad had bought two tables on Cee-Vid's behalf, but the seats were already divvied up among various members of his staff. Which left the seats at the tables his grandfather had gotten on behalf of the family ranch.

Squire had called Justin personally to command his attendance. Just because they hadn't expected him to still be in town when the tickets had been purchased months ago didn't mean that Justin wasn't expected to attend now. He was a Clay. And Clays had always shown their support for the hospital.

So Justin had borrowed the suit coat, bought a tie at Classic Charms on his lunch break that afternoon and here he was.

He stepped through the heavy plastic sheeting that served as the doorway for the party tent just as the attendees—at least two hundred, he was guessing—started clapping.

His aunt Rebecca was standing at the podium on the raised dais. She'd obviously just finished her speech, and he made his way past the empty dance floor area and around the perimeter of the tent to the table in the front row bearing a number four on the stand in the center of it. There was only one empty seat. It faced away from the dais and would have him looking back across the rest of the tables. Feeling self-conscious, he quickly crossed in front of the dais, yanked out the chair and sat.

"You're late," his cousin Casey said out the side of his mouth. "How'd you rate?".

Justin smiled across the table at his grandfather and grandmother, who were seated directly opposite him and Casey. Squire's gaze was steely; Gloria's smile was much more forgiving. "Lost track of time working."

It was partly true. The other part was having to clean up puppy poop, because the puppy had managed to get herself out of the temporary pen he'd fashioned in the living room of his apartment.

"Must be nice," Casey muttered and started clapping again when Jane elbowed him in the side.

Justin couldn't count the number of similar events he'd attended in Boston on behalf of CNJ. The company was always sponsoring one thing or another, and Charles wanted those he considered his key people to be familiar faces at them. Justin even had several custom-made suits hanging in his closet back in Boston. But he was happier wearing his borrowed suit coat from Jake.

It didn't hold a speck of Gillian's influence.

Finally, the applause died down. Rebecca thanked everyone for their support—which spurred another round of applause—and announced that the main course was being served.

That's when Justin noticed the catering crew positioned around the tent. At Rebecca's signal, they began pulling china plates from big metal carts. Salads and rolls were already on the tables.

"Where'd the catering come from?" The fancy carts

made the thing Tabby had used for the tree lighting seem like a toy.

"Cheyenne." His cousin Courtney was sitting on his other side. She was an RN at the hospital. "They came up with a ton of equipment and used the hospital kitchen to finish up. I heard it was a huge task to coordinate."

"Impressive." There was at least one server per table, so delivering the meals was accomplished with remarkable efficiency. Justin hoped the rest of the evening went with similar speed.

Mostly because he'd just spotted Tabby sitting one row over. She wasn't facing him. All he got was the fine line of her profile. But that was enough.

It had been a week since Gillian had come to town, just long enough to rain her particular brand of chaos all over his life. He had a no-name puppy that howled at night unless he let her sleep on his bed. No matter how often he corrected them, he still had people all over town thinking he was engaged to be married. And he had a landlord named Tabby who treated him like a stranger.

No, he corrected himself, as he watched her smile and converse with the other people seated around her. She treated strangers with more warmth than she offered him.

It was even worse than it had been four years ago, when he'd betrayed their entire friendship by getting her into bed.

Then, he'd felt like the biggest crumb on the planet.

Now, he was just pissed. Plain and simple.

She believed he'd lied. She'd rather believe the baloney that Gillian had spewed than the guy she'd known her whole life.

What the hell kind of friendship was that?

Courtney kicked him lightly beneath the table. "You're scowling," she said under her breath.

He wiped the frown off his face and realized everyone at his table had nearly finished their meal while he'd been sitting there fuming. He stabbed his fork into the salmon like it still needed killing and ate enough to avoid a questioning look from the server when she picked up his plate along with the others. It was replaced in short order with dessert—an assortment of crème brûlée, chocolate mousse and some little fruit tart—that he had no interest in, either. But before he could push it away, Courtney stole the entire lot, smiling innocently.

People were starting to move around the room, anyway, making visits to the bars spaced along one side of the heated tent, and he excused himself and went to the nearest one. He handed over one of the red tickets in exchange for a neat shot of whiskey that he tossed back in one gulp. Then he traded his second ticket for a bottle of beer.

When he looked around again, Tabby was no longer sitting at the table with her brother and his cousin Leandra, but he spotted her quickly enough in the center of the dance floor, where she stood out like a white beacon among a sea of little black dresses.

There was a DJ spinning music. It had been pretty much in the background through dinner, but now that the meal was over, the volume and pace had picked up, and Justin watched her dance. It took him a minute to realize the guy she was dancing with was Scott Brown from the hospital lab.

It was the lack of pale green scrubs, he decided.

Someone clapped him on the shoulder. "Yo, Justin. Heard you got hitched. Congratulations, man."

He just shook his head and shook off the hand. "Not married," he said. "Not getting married, either." He waded his way to the center of the dance floor, stopping next to Scott and Tabby. "Mind if I cut in?"

Scott looked surprised, but he started to move aside.

Tabby, on the other hand, gave Justin a searing look. "I mind," she said and quickly linked her hands behind Scott's neck.

Justin watched the other man's hands slide down the shimmering white fabric covering her back and took a long pull on his beer. Tabby's dress reached her thighs, leaving a whole lot of long, shapely leg uncovered.

She definitely didn't have skinned knees anymore.

The fact that people were having to dance around him didn't faze him in the least. "Guess I'll just wait, then," he said, meeting Tabby's fuming eyes with his own.

It was obvious as hell that Scott recognized he was caught in the middle of some sort of skirmish. And equally obvious to Justin that the other man wasn't particularly bothered by that fact.

Not if the guy's hands wrapped around Tabby's waist were anything to go by.

Fortunately, the song ended fairly quickly. During the commotion of people moving on and off the dance floor as the next song cranked up, Scott murmured something close to Tabby's ear that Justin couldn't hear and moved away from them.

Justin grabbed Tabby's hand before she could follow and yanked her close. "Whispering sweet nothings to you already?"

Her body was as stiff as a board, and the grimace of a smile she gave him was just as bad. "Whether he is or isn't, it's none of *your* business. You're bruising my wrist."

"I'm not holding you that tight," he retorted. But he lightened his grip all the same. Not enough to let her weasel out of it—a tactic she immediately tried. When she failed, she planted her sharp, high heel on the toe of his shoe. "Play nice," he warned. "At least for the benefit of the people watching."

She turned up her nose and looked away.

He wasn't able to shake some feeling back into his foot, though he wanted to. She clearly didn't care if *she* left bruises. "I'm the one who has a right to be mad."

She let out a disgusted sound, then turned on a brilliant smile as another dancing couple brushed by them. "Dee Crowder. Honest to Pete, you're the prettiest woman here tonight. I've never seen you look better."

The short, curly-headed blonde beamed back at Tabby. She taught elementary school along with one of Justin's cousins. But she was dancing with a balding man Justin didn't recognize. "The wonders of an engagement ring." Dee waggled her finger on which a diamond ring sparkled.

Tabby seemed to forget the need to mimic a wooden plank at the sight of the ring. "Oh, my goodness! You two are engaged?"

Dee nodded and her curls bounced. "Joe proposed on Thanksgiving Day."

Tabby laughed and gave the balding guy a pointed look. "It's about *time* y'all got your act together."

"Joe felt he needed to go to the school board first."

Justin's curiosity got the better of him. His mom was head of the school board. "School board? What for?"

Tabby blinked. "Oh. Sorry. I guess if you spent more time in Weaver, you'd have met." She delivered the jab along with the introduction. "Joe Gage. Principal at the elementary school. Justin Clay."

The balding guy stretched out a hand, which meant Justin had to release his grip on Tabby so he could reciprocate. "Nice to meet you. My mom used to teach at the elementary school. Hope Clay."

"Hope is your mom? She's a good lady." Joe dropped his arm over Dee's shoulder. She was nodding enthusiastically.

"Hope's one of the only voices of reason on the board," Dee said. "She thought it was ridiculous that Joe needed their permission before he proposed to me. Just because I teach at his school."

"It wasn't permission so much as hoping to avoid a gossip scandal," Joe said wryly. "You know what this town is like."

"Well, I for one couldn't be happier for the two of you," Tabby said. "Have you set a date?"

"It won't be until summer," Dee said. "After the school year is finished."

"Guess you'll have to find a new name for your poker group," Tabby said with a laugh.

Dee laughed, too, and swung back into Joe's arms. The couple two-stepped off to the latest song the DJ was playing.

Which left Tabby and Justin standing, again, in the middle of the dance floor.

"*You're* the prettiest woman here tonight," he said abruptly. "And for the record, I've never once lied to you. Not about Gillian. Not about anything. Not in our entire lives." Then, before she could respond, he turned and walked off the dance floor.

Scott was there waiting, two drinks in his hands.

"You hurt her, you'll answer to me," Justin said softly as he passed him, and he didn't stop until he'd left the tent altogether.

Tabby's cheeks felt as though they were on fire as she watched Justin walk away, leaving her standing there by herself in the middle of the dance floor.

The last time she'd felt remotely like this had been four years ago. At least then there had been no one to witness it.

She saw Scott on the periphery of the dance floor. A perfectly nice guy who deserved a girl equally as nice. Equally as interested.

Someone entirely different from Tabby.

She sighed and headed toward him. "Scott, I'm sorry, but I—" She stopped when he pushed two drinks into her hands.

"Dr. Clay's calling out her lab rats," he said, making her realize that Rebecca had taken the podium again and was calling up various members of the hospital staff. "Shouldn't take long."

Tabby smiled weakly and gave a last glance toward the tent's entrance. She wasn't going to walk out on Scott without at least explaining first. Which meant she was stuck there, at least for now.

"It's so exciting, isn't it?" Wyatt's girlfriend, Kristen, came up to stand next to Tabby.

Tabby shook herself a little and looked at the young woman. "I'm sorry. What's exciting?"

Kristen gave her an odd look. "Vivian Templeton's donation." She raised her eyebrows a little. "For the lab? It puts them over the top of what they needed to raise."

"Oh, right." Tabby smiled, even though she didn't have a clue. "It's very exciting."

"I wonder why she didn't come tonight," Kristen went on, apparently satisfied with Tabby's level of excitement. "If *I* were going to donate a couple million dollars to something, I sure would want to show my face." She giggled. "If I ever even had a couple million dollars. Talk about a fantasy, right?"

"Right."

Kristen soon went off in search of Wyatt, and since Scott was still standing on the dais along with the other lab staff, Tabby found an abandoned table and set down the drinks. Then she went out to the table where Sally was still sitting and retrieved her coat. "If Scott asks, tell him I went to powder my nose, will you?"

"Sure."

It was just an excuse. She made her way around the tent, hoping for some sign of Justin.

She didn't see him. Nor did she see that old truck he was using in the hospital parking lot.

Finally, she gave up and went back into the tent, where the DJ had started up again. The music was even louder, and Tabby wasn't surprised to see some people starting to make their exit. She stepped aside to wait while they retrieved coats and scarves from the racks behind Sally's table.

"Tabby, honey." Hope stopped in surprise at the sight of her. "Are you leaving, too?"

She glanced down at her coat that she hadn't yet removed. "Uh, no. Not just yet." She'd never felt awkward around Justin's mother in the past, and she hated feeling that way now. She pushed her fists into the side pockets. "That was quite some news about Mrs. Templeton's donation."

"Wasn't it?" Hope smiled slightly and held out her arms when Tristan came back with her long wool coat. She smiled up at him as he helped her on with it. "I thought Squire was going to choke on the news, though. Evidently, he was already up in arms because of the Christmas party Vivian's invited all of the family to. Courtney told me the only reason he didn't get up and leave tonight after the donation announcement was because Gloria hissed at him to sit back down."

"Want me to go warm up the car?"

Hope shook her head at Tristan. "No need. I'm too anxious to get out of these high heels." She stuck out her elegantly shod foot from beneath the hem of her long, swinging coat. "I love an excuse to get all dressed up, but there's always a cost."

"Yeah. To my wallet," Tristan drawled. He gave a quick a wink and the two of them headed off.

Sighing faintly, Tabby pulled aside the heavy plastic doorway and went back into the tent. She didn't have to feign a headache when she finally found Scott where he was standing with a bunch of folks from the hospital. Her head was pounding for real.

He took one look at the coat she was still wearing and peeled himself away from the others. "I wondered where you'd gotten to. You all right?"

"Just too much wine and music. Would you mind if I called it a night?"

He shook his head. "Of course not. Let me tell Wyatt we're leaving."

"You don't have to go. I'm practically around the corner."

"You're not walking home."

She could tell from his expression there was no point in arguing. And again, she knew he deserved better company than he'd gotten from her.

Which was exactly what she told him when they pulled up in front of her triplex a short while later. "I'm sorry. You should go back to the fund-raiser," she told him. "You have a lot to celebrate tonight."

"Definitely was a surprise about that Templeton lady's donation." He smiled slightly, obviously noticing her hand on the door handle. "Mind if I ask you a question?"

"Of course not."

"What's going on between you and Justin?"

"Nothing." She quickly looked away from the sight of his old truck parked on the street ahead of them. "Nothing good, anyway."

"So you cutting the night short doesn't have anything to do with him?"

She opened her mouth to say it didn't. But the words wouldn't come. "I'm sorry," she said again. "We just, um, Justin and I used to be friends."

Scott shifted, stretching his hand over the back of her seat. "Sure about that? Because it felt to me like there wasn't a lot of *used to be* going on between the two of you. What it felt like was that there was a whole lot going on right now."

Her cheeks heated. "It's not like that."

He waited a beat. Then he shrugged. "Okay. It's not like it's in my best interest to convince you otherwise." His fingertips toyed with the ends of her hair. "But I figure if we're going to try this again sometime—without Wyatt and his sweet nitwit of a girlfriend—I'd just as soon know what kind of odds I'm looking at."

"Why would you even want to go out with me again?"

"Beautiful. *Not* a nitwit." He chuckled. "Two positives right there."

"You're hard not to like," she admitted ruefully. "But—"

"But you're hung up on the guy who *used* to be your friend."

She exhaled. "Scott—"

"I know. I'm a nice guy. But." He suddenly leaned forward and kissed her.

She was so surprised, all she did was sit there, and then he sat back again.

"That wasn't too bad, was it?"

It hadn't set rockets off inside her, but it hadn't exactly been like kissing a toad, either. "No."

"So, if you decide what used to be really is a used to be, give me a call."

She smiled and pushed open the car door. "G'night, Scott."

"Night, Tabby."

He didn't drive away until she unlocked her front door and went inside. Not bothering to turn on a light, she dropped her keys on the table by the door and discarded her coat on the couch before going to stand in front of the window. There was a streetlight on the corner that cast its glow wide enough to encompass Justin's truck sitting in front of the triplex.

Before she could talk herself out of it, she dashed

back outside, trotted past Mrs. Wachowski's dark windows and knocked on his door.

The second she did, the puppy started barking.

Then she heard Justin telling the dog to be quiet, and he yanked open the door. "What?"

She looked from the squirming puppy he was holding to his annoyed face.

Then she stepped close, pulled his head down and pressed her mouth to his.

He yanked back, staring at her like she'd lost her mind. "What the hell was that for?"

"Rockets," she snapped, and turning on her heel, raced back to her apartment.

She slammed the door behind her and flipped the lock.

Even through the walls, she could hear the puppy still barking.

"Damn rockets," she said thickly.

She stomped into her studio, snatched up the blizzard painting that she'd never been able to part with and added it to the pile waiting to be shipped off to Bolieux.

Then she sat down on the floor and cried.

Chapter Ten

"Tabby," Bubba barked from the kitchen, drawing her attention away from the coffee brewer she was cleaning. "Phone."

She set down the scrub brush, peeled off her rubber gloves and went into the kitchen. It was Monday afternoon, past closing time, but she and Bubba were taking care of some of the heavy-duty cleaning chores. She grabbed the receiver where it was hanging loose by the twisting, coiled cord. "Hello?"

"Tabby, dear. I'm so sorry to bother you at work."

She recognized the voice immediately. "Mrs. Wachowski. What's wrong?"

"It's Justin's puppy, I'm afraid. She's just howling so miserably. Has been all afternoon. I'm afraid she's going to make herself ill. I tried calling Justin at the hospital, but I couldn't reach him. I don't know what else to do."

Tabby held back a sigh. Since she'd kissed him the other night, she hadn't seen or heard from him.

As if she'd needed *more* proof of his romantic disinterest.

"I'll take care of it, Mrs. Wachowski."

"You're such a sweet girl. I knew you would, dear."

After she hung up, she let the sigh loose. She looked at Bubba, whose upper body was nearly engulfed by the oven he was repairing. "I have to run home for a few minutes," she told him and got only a few metallic bangs in response.

She had her car with her because she'd planned to ship the paintings after she was finished at the diner, so running back to the triplex took even less time than usual. As soon as she parked in the driveway, she could hear the puppy's sharp, frantic yipping.

She found the spare keys she kept for the other two units in her bedroom dresser and let herself in through Justin's door.

He'd attempted to make a temporary cardboard pen for the puppy in the living room. That was immediately obvious. Equally obvious, though, was the fact that the creative little dog had managed to eat her way through it. There were scraps of half-eaten cardboard everywhere, as well as what looked like pillow stuffing and a shredded leash.

"Oh, Beastie," Tabby murmured and caught the puppy before she could dash out the open door. She picked up the dog, who was no longer barking shrilly but lavishing her chin with wet licks, and turned her back on the mess. She relocked the door behind her and set the puppy on the brown grass, hoping that she'd tinkle.

Instead, the animal started to take off after a blowing leaf, and Tabby caught her up again just in time to keep her from running into the street. "You need a new leash. A chain one this time."

With the dog standing on her passenger seat, front

paws propped on the dashboard, Tabby drove to her brother's vet practice. His office manager told Tabby he was out on a call, but she was still able to buy a leash there, a tie chain and a few chew toys. Then she drove back to the diner and fixed Beastie up with the chain outside the rear door.

"It's not perfect," she said, crouching down beside the little dog to scratch her ears. "But you've been cooped up inside long enough. Now you can chase all the leaves you want while I finish up here, and the chain will keep you from running out where you're not supposed to be." The puppy yapped and bounced up to lick Tabby's face again, then snatched the squeaky chew toy when Tabby tossed it.

With the dog happily occupied, she went inside.

Bubba had finished the oven repair and had taken up where Tabby had left off on the coffee brewer.

"I can finish that if you want to take off."

"Nah. Nearly done, anyway." He picked up a jug of water and poured it in the brewer. "Run a few gallons of water through it, she's good as new."

Tabby sat on a stool. "And the oven? You think the new heating element will keep it going for a while, or is it time to start thinking replacement?" The oven had been ancient even when Tabby began working at the diner so many years ago. "With the space it takes up, we could have something newer and a lot more efficient."

He grunted in agreement. "Yeah. But newer ain't always better. 'N' you've been baking cinnamon rolls in there for more years than I remember."

"Ruby told me she bought that oven secondhand the very first year she turned a profit on this place. Back then she used it for everything. Not just the rolls." Tabby propped her chin on her hand, staring blindly at the diner around her. "Maybe the reason the rolls are so popular is because I'm still using her old oven."

Bubba snorted and poured another jug of water through the brewer. "Maybe the reason is 'cause you make great rolls and any old oven would do."

She chewed the inside of her lip. "So, you think it might be time to give up on old...habits?"

He gave her a strange look. "I'm saying any working oven'll do." He finished draining the brewer one last time and dumped the water down the sink. "And the brewer's done, so I'm outta here, unless you got somethin' else you need me to do."

She shook her head. You go on, Bubba." She knew he was cooking for Vivian Templeton that evening. "Thanks."

He lifted his hand in a wave and disappeared through the swinging doors to the kitchen. A moment later, she heard the back door slam shut. It opened a second later, though. "You know you got a pooch chained up out here," he yelled.

"Yes, I do, Bubba. See you in the morning."

Her answer was the slam of the metal door again.

She pushed off the stool and finished tidying up, then went to check on the dog. Beastie had managed to wind her chain around the base of the picnic table, limiting her range. "You're making things hard on yourself, little girl. Trust me. I recognize the tendency." She unclipped the puppy from the chain and carried her to the car, setting her on the passenger seat again. "Now you've got to behave," she warned. "Just because my car is old doesn't mean I want you chewing or peeing on the seats."

The puppy cocked her head then yipped and jumped onto Tabby's lap.

"Wish everyone were as agreeable as you." Tabby kissed the dog's silky head and set her aside again before driving all the way to the shipping office in Braden. With the leashed dog by her side, she went inside and mailed off her paintings. Then she picked up some Chinese takeout for her supper and drove back to Weaver, though she had to stop halfway there to put the takeout containers in the trunk, because Beastie kept trying to nuzzle her way into them.

The sun was nearly down by the time she got home. Justin's truck was parked in front of the triplex.

She blew out a breath as she pushed open the car door and gathered the puppy in her arms. "Come on, little girl. Time for you to go home." She nudged the car door closed with her hip, walked reluctantly to the Justin's apartment and knocked.

He answered immediately, reminding her much too vividly of the last time she'd knocked on his door. "Here." She held the puppy out to him. "Mrs. Wachowski called me about the barking."

"She told me."

"Get a kennel cage," she advised. "Before she chews her way through everything you own. She also needs toys. And her shots if she hasn't had them yet."

"How would I know if she's had her shots?"

She smiled tightly. "Ask Gillian." She started to walk away. Then swore under her breath and looked back at him. "I can watch the dog for you in the afternoon after I close up the diner. She's a baby. She's lonely. And I don't particularly want to have to replace the furniture for the next renter." She continued on her way.

"Tabby—"

Even though she'd been determined not to react to him, she felt her nerves tighten. "Don't have time to talk," she lied. "I'm on my way over to my parents'."

"You didn't used to be a coward."

Her jaw tightened. If she were a coward, she never would have kissed him the way she had the other night. She was, however, an idiot for having done so. Even now, her skin felt as though it was burning with humiliation beneath her clothes. But she turned and faced him again, propping her hand on her hip impatiently. "What?"

"Erik added you to the bank account for the diner."

It was the very last thing she expected him to say. "What?"

"All you need to do is sign a card at the bank tomorrow."

She dropped her hand from her hip. "What are you talking about?"

"The diner."

"I know you mean the diner! Why would he do that? Everything worked perfectly well the way it was."

"Because I told him it was stupid when you ran everything else there, and he agreed. Why are you looking all pissed off?" He closed the puppy inside and headed toward her on the sidewalk. "I thought you'd be happy. You don't have to wait on Erik every time you need to pay a bill."

"How many times do I have to say that our system worked just fine? And why are you suddenly acting interested in the way the diner is run?"

"I thought you'd be happy," he repeated. "Dammit, Tabby, what do you want from me? You act like you still hate me. Then you think I lied about Gillian. Then you plant that…that kiss—"

"It was a mistake," she said quickly, before he could go any further. "A stupid mistake."

"But—"

"I've really got to go. You know how mom hates dinner to be late." A ridiculous statement, considering her mother's easygoing personality. Tabby continued backing away. "Evan can get you a kennel. Maybe even loan you one while you're here."

"Tabby—"

She turned on her heel and jogged the short distance to her car, proving she really was a coward after all. "I'll talk to Erik about the bank account," she said and quickly got in, cranking the engine so hard a belch of smoke came out the tailpipe.

She backed out onto the street and drove away.

She saw the red glow of his cigarette before she made out the shape of him sitting in the dark on her front porch.

She'd killed as much time at her folks' house as she could without drawing suspicion. As it was, while she helped her mother wrap Christmas gifts, she'd had to derail Jolie's none-too-subtle remarks about "things" she'd been hearing around town concerning Tabby and Justin. Hiding out there any longer than she had would only have made it worse. It was nearly ten and her parents knew she was the poster child for early to bed, early to rise.

And, evidently, Tabby could only be a coward for so long before even she found herself intolerable.

She closed the car door and clasped the sides of her

coat together in front of her, walking slowly toward him. "You don't seem to be giving them up."

The red glow moved upward and flared briefly as he took a drag. "Don't seem to be," he agreed. "You going to talk to me now, or what?"

It was annoying how quickly her throat went tight.

She reached the porch step and sat down beside him. The second she did, she felt a wet canine nose nudge at her hand. "Hi, Beastie." The puppy climbed onto her lap, and Tabby rubbed her fingertips against her smooth coat.

"It's a fitting name," he said. "She ate one of my shoes this afternoon."

"Get a proper kennel cage."

"I did. She figured out how to unfasten the latch."

"Admittedly brilliant on her part." The dog started crawling up her chest. "But more likely that you didn't fasten the latch properly."

"You want to tell me what that was about the other night?"

She shook her head, which, given the darkness and the fact that her porch light wasn't on, was pretty useless as a form of communication. "Not really." Then she sighed and pushed to her feet, still holding the pup. "I don't know how long you've been sitting there, but my butt is already freezing." She stepped around him and unlocked her front door. "If you're coming in, leave the cigarette outside."

A moment later, he followed her inside, squinting a little at the light she turned on. She set the dog on the floor. "Be nice."

"That a warning for the dog or for me?"

She pulled off her coat and dropped it over one of the

couch arms, and then toed off her tennis shoes. "Maybe for all three of us. You want something to drink?"

"What're you offering?" He removed his leather jacket and left it on top of her coat.

"Arsenic?" She smiled thinly and went into the kitchen. "I have water and—" she pulled open the refrigerator door "—diet soda and one beer." She reached for the beer before he even answered.

"Beer."

She closed the refrigerator and twisted off the cap, handing him the bottle. Then she filled a cereal bowl with some water and set it on the floor for Beastie. "I'm sorry about the other night," she said abruptly. She made a face. "Kissing you like that. It was—" Dumb? Foolish? Fruitless? "Was, um, wildly inappropriate."

He straddled one of her bar stools. His violet eyes studied her while he took a drink from the bottle. "Why?" he asked when he lowered it.

"Why what?"

"Why inappropriate?"

She pressed her tongue against her teeth, searching for an answer. "Because."

He raised his eyebrows. "Because…why?"

She let out a breath and left the kitchen, restlessly going down the hall into her studio.

He followed, scooping up Beastie when she tried to go between his feet. Holding the dog, he leaned his shoulder against the doorjamb. She didn't know if he did it to block her exit or not, but the result was the same either way. She plucked several brushes out of the empty can where she'd left them to dry and began organizing them.

"Tabby."

She abruptly swept all of the brushes into a drawer and slammed it shut. "It's inappropriate because we're not—" She didn't look at him as she waved her hand. "You know. Not that kind of friends. Kissing kind of friends."

He remained silent, which only added to the embarrassment burning through her.

She switched her restless attention to the closest stack of paintings against the wall. Her throat felt tighter than ever as she moved them needlessly from one wall to another.

Justin watched the overhead light shining on her dark hair as she worked. Until he'd messed things up with her four years ago, she'd been a staple in his life. But he wasn't a complete idiot. She was beautiful. He'd always been aware of that. But as she'd said, they weren't that kind of friends. So, aside from his enormous onetime transgression, he'd always done his best to ignore her appeal. Because that's the way she wanted it.

Or so he'd thought.

She'd moved the paintings back to their original places. There were only half the number he'd seen last time. As she crouched down and fussed with them, he could tell that the blizzard painting was gone.

"Maybe that's what our problem is," he said quietly.

She went still.

He set the dog on the floor and reached down to grab Tabby's hands, pulling her to her feet.

Her eyes were wide. Dark. And full of wariness.

"Pretending we weren't the kissing kind of friends," he added, just to be clear. Something in her gaze flickered, and he felt the resistance in her hands. "Don't pull away."

She didn't, though she spread her fingers, almost experimentally, as if she were still planning to. "Justin, this isn't a good idea."

"What isn't a good idea?"

Her fingers curled. "What, uh, whatever it is you're thinking about doing."

He could read her thoughts as clearly as his own.

And damn straight she knew what he was thinking.

He released one of her hands and slid his palm along her jaw. Felt her jerk a little, but not away from him. He pushed her chin up with his thumb and leaned closer. "I think it's one of the best ideas I've had in a really—" he leaned even closer "—really long time." Four years, at least.

He closed the last few inches of distance between them and pressed his mouth against hers.

He didn't close his eyes.

Nor did she.

So he saw in her eyes what he felt in the kiss.

The kick start of blood.

The sudden blast of heat.

The urgent desire for more.

He moved his hand, sliding it behind her neck, threading his fingers through her thick, silky hair, angling her head. Her eyes fluttered closed, and her hands roved over his shoulders, fingertips kneading. Then she made a soft sound, and her lips parted against his.

Whatever he'd planned—an experiment, a test, a challenge—went up in smoke. Any thought beyond getting more of Tabby Taggart was impossible.

More warm flesh beneath the sweater he dragged over her head.

More of the pulse beating like a wild thing below her ear lobe.

More of the sweeter-than-sweet taste of her tight nipple through the lace covering it. She inhaled deeply and yanked at his shirt so forcefully that he heard it rip and buttons pop. He dragged down the zipper on her jeans and pushed his hands inside.

She twined herself around him, gasping against his neck as he lifted her onto her messy worktable and buried himself inside her. She cried out, arching against him sharply as her sweet, hot spasms gloved him, luring him into oblivion.

Justin wasn't sure how long it was after that before his good sense started to return.

He was sure, however, that Tabby wasn't as slow in that regard as he was.

His heart was still pounding and the sweat on their bodies hadn't cooled before she was unwinding her legs and pushing away from him, reaching for her clothes that somehow had spread out from corner to corner of her studio.

"Tabby—"

She shook her head, throwing out her palm. "Whatever you're going to say, don't." She picked up her bra, took one look at the lace that had been torn in two and tossed it aside before yanking her sweater over her head, pulling it down past her bare thighs. "If I hear another apology from you after—" She broke off and waved the jeans she plucked off the floor. "I won't be responsible for what I do."

She might have ended up gloriously naked, but he hadn't gotten that far. He hitched up his jeans. "Well, then relax, because I'm *not* apologizing." He wasn't sure where the stamina came from after the sex storm that had just flattened him, but he was abruptly and wholly pissed. "You were more than willing, Tabbers. And neither one of us has the excuse of being drunk this time." Not that there really was any comparison to the last time.

Hell, after he'd unintentionally, drunkenly mumbled another woman's name to her four years ago, that particular party had screeched to a dead-as-a-doornail stop. There'd been no spectacular finish. No daunting fear that he might actually be in over his head where she was concerned. And damn sure no haunting suspicion that no woman was ever going to fit him as perfectly as Tabitha Taggart did.

Which was a suspicion that freaked him out more than anything else.

"Yes, well, I don't need pity sex from you, either," she said thickly as she left the room.

"What?" He followed her, stepping over his shirt on the floor as she headed down the short hall and into her bedroom. "Where the hell did you get *that* stupid idea?"

She didn't look at him. Just dumped her jeans on the bed and yanked open one of her dresser drawers to pull out a folded shirt. Then she went into the bathroom and slammed the door shut in his face.

His head started to pound. He matched it beat for beat with the palm of his hand against the wooden door. "Dammit, Tabby!"

"Go home, Justin." Maybe it was the door between them that made her voice sound thick. "Take Beastie with you."

He didn't want to go home. Didn't want to leave her.

The fact that she didn't want him, though, was too obvious to ignore.

"This isn't over," he warned through the door.

"There isn't anything *to* be over," she yelled back at him. "Do you want me to watch your dog in the afternoons or not?"

His head pounded even more. "Yes!"

Then he scooped up Beastie, who'd been chewing on his ankle, and looked the puppy in the eye. "God save me from freaking crazy females," he said through his teeth. "And that includes you, too."

Then he walked out.

Chapter Eleven

"Justin's here. He's asking to see you."

When Paulette made her announcement, Tabby didn't pull her hands out of the bread dough she was kneading. After the insanity in her studio the night before, she had been clinging to every shred of normalcy she could find.

Which, to her, meant baking rolls at Ruby's.

She was on her fifth batch even though it was the lunch rush and she should have been working the front along with the other servers.

"Just tell him to chain the dog up out back until I'm finished here," she told Paulette.

"He doesn't have a dog with him."

"Then tell him I'll pick her up at his place when I'm through. So I hope he's got her contained in her kennel."

Paulette shrugged, adjusting her apron around her waist and disappearing through the swinging doors.

"You punishing that bread dough for something?"

Tabby didn't look up. "Not now, Bubba."

"Just sayin'." He slapped a burger on the grill and reached up to the pass-through to grab the next order. "You get one of Miz Templeton's party invitations?"

She shook her head. "Nope." Which was fine with her. The last fancy-dress event she'd attended had been the hospital fund-raiser. Her emotions had been spiraling since.

The swinging door pushed open again. "Paulette—"

"I am not Paulette."

Tabby's fingertips dug into the dough. She glanced at Justin standing in the doorway and looked away just as quickly. He was wearing jeans and a leather jacket. A CNJ-logoed ball cap covered his head, the bill pulled low over his eyes. But the memory of his thick blond hair standing in spikes because of her fingers twisting through it was just as vivid in her mind as the reality of him now. "I told you last night I'd take care of Beastie."

"That's about the *only* thing you told me last night," he countered. He took another step farther into the kitchen, allowing the door to swing shut behind him.

She dashed more flour over the sticky dough. She was excruciatingly aware that Bubba was watching the two of them. "It was the only thing that needed to be said."

He snorted and moved next to the rolling cart where she was working. "What happened was unexpected, but not the end of the world," he said under his breath. "You're acting like an outraged virgin or something."

Her face caught fire. She looked from him to Bubba, who was adding more burgers to the one already sizzling on the grill, and back to Justin again. "This is neither the time nor the place," she hissed.

"Then when *is* the time and place? You were gone before dawn this morning. You had the diner locked up tight when I came by before I went to work."

She faltered for half a moment. She hadn't heard him

come by this morning. "You're the one who wants me to keep the door here locked until opening. Or have you already forgotten?"

"I haven't forgotten anything."

She scooped up the heavy mound of dough, flipped it over and slapped it back down hard against the floury board. A cloud of white exploded over the front of Justin's clothes. "Give it time," she advised.

"You used to say exactly what was on your mind," he said, swiping his hand over his jeans. "What happened?"

You. She turned away from the dough that she was going to have to throw away because of the punishment she'd been giving it and tossed a clean towel at him. "When you finish slumming it here in Weaver, you'll go back to Boston and everything'll return to normal. You won't give a thought to this place until you come back for the next holiday. Is that clear enough now?"

His expression darkened. "This is my hometown, too, Tab. I've never once considered it *slumming.* If that's the word in your head, maybe that's how *you* feel!"

Her jaw loosened. "I love Weaver. I'm not the one who is always leaving it!"

"And why is that? Maybe you're really just afraid to go out and see what else the world has to offer. Instead you stay here, comfortable ruling your Ruby's roost, dabbling with your painting and playing *spinster* poker!"

The music coming from Bubba's ancient radio suddenly shot up in volume, startling them both. Tabby gave her cook a look.

Bubba gave her a look back. "Folks around town are

already talking about the two of you. You want to give 'em even more fuel?"

Her shoulders drooped. She went over to the sink and washed away the dough clinging to her fingers. She could feel Justin watching from behind her; it was like the point of a firebrand pressing between her shoulder blades.

Then she heard the scrape of his shoe, and a moment later the door was swinging hard after him.

She blinked against the burning behind her eyes, turned off the water and blindly reached for the paper towels.

Bubba handed the roll to her.

She avoided his concerned look and tore off a few sheets to dry her hands.

"Wanna tell ol' Bubba what that was about?"

She shook her head and went over to the worktable, where she scraped the dough into the trash barrel.

"Ever consider just telling the guy how you feel?"

She frowned, continuing to scrape the wooden board with the edge of her metal spatula. "I don't know what you mean."

"Yes, you do. You got it bad for the boss. Looks like he's got it bad for you, too."

Her jaw ached from clenching it. "I can tell you that he definitely does not."

"Then what happened last night between the two of you? 'Cause something sure as shootin' did."

"Nothing happened," she lied. Because as much as she loved Bubba Bumble, she wasn't about to tell him what had happened the night before. "Your burgers are starting to burn."

They weren't.

But Bubba mercifully turned his attention back to his grill, anyway. "So, about that party of Miz Templeton's," he said, sounding faintly diffident—which was so entirely out of character for Bubba that it succeeded in penetrating Tabby's misery.

"What about it?"

"She invited me. Sent me one of her fancy invitations and everything." He pulled something from his pocket and tossed it toward her.

She wasn't quick enough to catch it. Kneeling down, she picked up the ivory square from the floor and unfolded it. "Fancier than a wedding invitation," she murmured, waving the engraved card between her fingers.

He made a face, deftly assembling the hamburgers and plating them alongside steaming-hot French fries before setting them on the pass-through. "Order up," he yelled, then looked back at Tabby. "I didn't expect her to invite me."

"Why wouldn't she? You've been cooking for her for a while now. Do you *want* to go?"

He glanced at the orders lined up in front of him and dumped more thin-sliced potatoes into the fryer. "If I don't, she might not ask me to cook for her anymore when Montrose is off. And the money's good."

"I doubt she'd do that."

He looked skeptical. "I don't know, Tabby. She's kind of a crazy old lady."

"So go, if you're worried about it. You can rent a tux in Braden, I'm sure. What's the problem?"

He cracked two eggs with one hand over the grill and pitched the shells in the trash without having to look. "Invitation says me and a guest."

For the first time all day, Tabby felt faintly amused.

"So you get to take a date. That's hardly a problem, Bubba. People all over this town are curious to see inside that mansion she's built."

He let out a disgusted grunt. "I don't wanna find a date. Some girl who'll want a *second* date."

"God forbid," she murmured drily.

"I was thinking maybe you'd go with me."

She raised her eyebrows. "Me?"

"Well, you wouldn't be expecting anything dumb from me, like flowers 'n' stuff. And you'd fit in there better than the ladies I know down at Jojo's."

Jojo's was a dive bar on the other end of town. "Thanks, I think."

"So? Party's Saturday night."

Even though she'd just been counting her blessings that she hadn't received an invitation, she smiled at him. "Sure, Bubba. Why not? I'm curious to see inside her mansion, too." At least there was no need to worry about any romantic complications. The man was like a rough-edged, well-meaning uncle.

And maybe, just maybe, it would give her an opportunity to think about something *other* than Justin.

When the lunch rush abated, she walked home, leaving Paulette to close up the restaurant. It started snowing before she got there, and by the time she'd changed into warmer clothes and liberated Beastie from the kennel cage Justin had procured, the ground was covered in a solid layer of white. This was a source of curiosity to Beastie, who approached the whole matter with obvious wariness before she found a squatworthy corner of the yard. But once she'd done her business, the mystery of the white stuff became a sudden playground, and it took Tabby quite some time before she was able to corral the mischievous pup and go inside.

She called her mom for wardrobe guidance for the Templeton party while she stood guard over the dog wolfing down puppy kibble and water. "Bubba's invitation said black tie. That's fancier than the fund-raiser was, and I had a heck of a time finding a dress for *that*. What's Mrs. Templeton thinking, anyway? This is Weaver. We don't do black tie."

Jolie laughed. "My encounters with Vivian Templeton make me believe that she expects Weaver to adjust to her rather than the other way around. I'm just glad that your father and I had an honest reason to decline the invitation we received, since he needs to be in Cheyenne this weekend. I know she only sent the invitation because I did her gown. From what I've heard, it's mostly family members she's inviting."

The Clays and the Templetons. That included Justin.

Tabby pushed aside the troublesome thought. "Bubba figures he needs to go in order to stay in her good graces," she told her mother. "I wonder if I could just rent a gown somewhere."

"Tabby! You're not going to rent a gown."

"What? Anything else seems silly when I'll only be wearing it a few hours. Bubba only needs me as his plus one. I'm hardly out to impress anyone." Especially Justin. *If* he was going to be there. Which he probably wouldn't be, anyway.

She pinched the bridge of her nose in a vain attempt to stanch her mental nonsense.

"And I've heard there are places that rent gowns," she continued. "Same as guys rent tuxedos. You don't think anything about that."

"There's nothing wrong with renting a gown if you need to," Jolie said. "But I'm a seamstress, for heaven's sake. With a daughter who has never needed a formal gown. Not even for her high school prom."

"I didn't go to prom." She'd stayed home, hiding her misery beneath an I-don't-care-about-stupid-dances attitude because Justin had taken Collette.

"My point exactly," Jolie said. "Come to the house this afternoon. We'll work up a design before dinner."

"What about Vivian's gown?"

"Already finished. See you soon." Without waiting for Tabby to offer another argument, her mother ended the call.

Tabby hung up her phone and looked down at Beastie. The puppy was lying across the toes of her boots, evidently tuckered after romping in the snow and filling her stomach. "You're lucky," Tabby said to the dog. "You never need to worry about this sort of thing."

The dog's ears didn't even twitch. She just continued snoring softly.

"Well, at least you're not chewing up anything," Tabby said.

It wasn't much. But it was something.

Justin stared at the nearly indecipherable note taped to his front door. Obviously Tabby's handwriting. Aside from the word *Beastie*, there was little that he could make out in the rest of the sentence.

He crumpled the note and went inside. He knew she wasn't home. He didn't put it past her not to answer the door if he knocked, but her car was gone.

He stepped around the empty kennel cage and threw himself down on the couch, not bothering to remove his jacket, and closed his eyes. He had less than a month left before he needed to present the finished report to Charles, but he still had twice that many days' worth of materials to get through.

Didn't help that every time he tried to concentrate on the work, he kept thinking about Tabby.

At this rate, he should have just stayed in Boston.

He'd have been equally unproductive, but at least he wouldn't have gotten tangled up with her like he had.

His cell phone vibrated, and he pulled it out of his pocket, wearily focusing on the display. It was his mother.

He hesitated for a moment, then swore softly and answered. "Hey, Mom."

"*What* is going on with you and Tabby?"

He sat up straighter. "What? Nothing."

"Then why have I been hearing all day about some fight the two of you had at Ruby's?"

God help him. "It wasn't a fight."

"I don't know what to make of all this, honey. First that business about being engaged to Gillian. Now all this with Tabby."

"There's no *all this*!" He pushed to his feet and paced around the kennel cage, because evidently he couldn't lie to his mother when he was seated.

"She's like a daughter to me, Justin. I won't tolerate any dissension between the two of you, any more than I would between you and your brother."

If only it were that easy. "There's no dissension."

"See that there isn't," she said crisply. "I don't want to be countering gossip about you long after you've returned to Boston, and you know that's what I'll be doing if people around town don't find something more interesting to speculate about."

"There's no dissension," he repeated.

"Fine." Her tone warmed a little. "Why don't you come out for dinner tonight?"

"I can't." That, at least, was the truth. "I've got too much work to do." He'd only come home long enough to see to the dog.

Who wasn't even there.

He heard his mother sigh. "Well, make sure you eat something," she said. "I know how you can get when you're involved in a project. And make sure you carve out at least a few hours Saturday evening."

"What's going on Saturday evening?"

"Vivian Templeton's Christmas party. I told you about it the last time we talked."

"Right." He'd gotten the invitation. Tossed it somewhere. "I don't even know the lady. Why is it you want me to go?"

"Because, regardless of what your grandfather wants us to think, it's the polite thing to do. She's just dropped a ton of money on the hospital. The woman is family whether Squire wants to admit it or not, and we're going to act like it."

Justin still didn't think his presence would matter to Vivian Templeton one way or another. But it obviously mattered to his mother. And he didn't need to be at cross-purposes with yet another female. "I can spare a few hours."

"You'll need a tux."

He managed not to swear out loud. Tuxedos in Weaver were about the most outlandish thing that he could imagine. "Fine."

"Justin—"

"I'll have a tux," he assured her, containing his impatience with an effort. "You get the same promise from Erik?"

"Erik is Izzy's problem," Hope said. "But I'm sure she'll succeed."

No doubt. His brother would turn cartwheels in a tutu for his wife, particularly now that she was pregnant with their child.

Justin's phone vibrated in his hand, alerting him to another call. "Got another call, Mom. If I don't see you before then, I'll see you Saturday."

"All right. I love you, honey."

"You, too." More interested in getting off the hook with her while he was still in her good graces than anything else, he switched calls. "Yes?"

"Justin, my boy! Charles here. How is the report coming?"

Justin grimaced. Sometimes you were the bug. Sometimes you were the windshield. These days, he was feeling like he was both. "It's coming, Charles."

"I don't have to remind you what it'll mean to the company if you get it completed on time."

"I know." He opened the door and looked out at the falling snow. He'd forgotten that it could actually be a pretty sight. But what really caught his attention was the car pulling into the driveway.

Tabby's car.

"Can I ask you a favor, Charles?"

"As long as it doesn't cost me a few more million dollars."

"Can you send someone over to my apartment?

Someone other than Gillian. Strangely enough, I need to have a tux shipped here by Saturday."

"My secretary can take care of it."

"Thanks. If there's nothing else you needed, I've got a report to get back to."

"That's what I like to hear, my boy. Exactly what I like to hear."

Justin ended the call, pocketing the phone as he stepped off the porch and headed toward Tabby's vehicle. The moment she opened the car door, the puppy escaped, racing toward him so fast she practically tripped over her own long ears.

He scooped her up, and she licked his face a few times before scrabbling at him to be let back down again. The second he did so, she was off like a bolt toward Tabby, who was already on her porch, unlocking the door.

He followed the dog, hoping to make it before Tabby could close the door in his face.

And he would have, too. If his shoe hadn't landed in a pile of dog poop, sending him sliding in the slick snow.

He landed flat on his back, the breath slamming out of him as he stared up at the flecks of white coming down at him from the solid gray sky.

Perfect. Just perfect.

"Oh, my goodness." Mrs. Wachowski opened her door and peered out at him lying half in and half out of the bushes lining the front of her unit. "I saw you through my window. Are you hurt?"

He coughed. "Besides my pride?" He winced when Beastie pounced on his chest. "I'll survive." He sat up and eyed Tabby's door. Which was now closed.

Probably locked again. At least against him.

"Ever have one of those days, Mrs. Wachowski?"

"Sure." She left her porch and bent over beside him, tucking her frail hand beneath his arm. He didn't need her assistance as he got to his feet, but he couldn't help appreciating her effort. "Then I finally retired from teaching history to hooligans like you and that Rasmussen boy, and they stopped." She dashed her hands over his shoulders, brushing away the clinging snow. "There you are. Right as rain. You're certain you're not hurt anywhere?"

He glanced at Tabby's closed door again. "Once I deal with the mess I'm in, I'll be fine."

She wrinkled her nose, obviously thinking he meant the dark smear on his shoe. "Fortunately, messes clean up." She patted his shoulder and returned to her door, going inside.

Justin exhaled and scraped his sole against the edge of the sidewalk as well as he could. Then he continued to Tabby's door and knocked.

The porch light flicked on, and she answered so immediately he wondered if she'd seen his ignominious tumble. "We need to talk."

"Not really." She brushed past him, pulling the door closed again. "I'm on my way out."

"You just got back."

"So?"

"Where are you going now?"

She lifted her eyebrows and headed toward her car. "I don't believe that's any of your business, actually."

"Got a call from my mother because she heard we'd been fighting at the diner. She's concerned about... dissension."

She stopped and looked back at him. "There's no dissension."

He rubbed the puppy's silky head where she'd tucked it under his chin. "That's what I told her."

"So we're both liars," he heard her mutter. "I knew this would happen."

He closed the distance between them. It was getting darker by the second. "There's an easy solution."

She gave him a disbelieving look. "Easy."

He continued, speaking over her. "Have an adult conversation with me for once about what's going on."

"We had sex," she said tightly. "And it was a mistake. That's what's going on."

"I don't think sex was a mistake. I think most everything that's happened since we had sex has been a mistake."

She looked away, dashing a snowflake off her face. "I feel like we're in the middle of a fishbowl," she muttered. "Mrs. Wachowski's watching us through her front window."

"And Mr. Rowe's pretending to sweep snow off his front porch while he looks this way. We are in a fishbowl. That doesn't change anything. We had sex, Tabby. I wasn't doing you some damn sort of favor. We kissed, and that's all she wrote. I thought you were right there with me, but I guess I was wrong."

Her gaze flicked up to his. She moistened her lips. "You weren't wrong," she said almost inaudibly.

Only the knowledge that they were being watched kept him from reaching for her. "Then what's the problem?"

"Besides not wanting to upset either one of our families? I don't want to get used to something that's not going to last."

He opened his mouth to argue the point but couldn't.

And her expression said she knew it. "You're going to finish your work soon and go back to Boston. And I'm going to be here."

"Come with me."

He didn't know where the words had come from, but they were out there now. And she was staring at him as if he'd suggested she move to Mars. "Go *with* you! What are you—"

"You can paint there," he said over her words. "Just as easily as you can paint here."

She blinked, going quiet for a moment. "Painting is my hobby," she finally said.

"One you're earning money doing."

"Yes. But I still enjoy it because it *is* a hobby. If I *had* to paint for my living?" She shook her head.

"Then don't paint!" Something was slipping through his fingers, and he wasn't even sure what it was. "Do something else. Anything else that you want to do. You can live with me. Or…or find a place of your own." That wasn't at all what he wanted, but if he just got her out there, he could sway her.

His gut tightened. He was pretty sure he could.

Her head tilted slightly, and her dark hair slid over her shoulder. She reached out and brushed her fingertips over Beastie's sleeping head. "I am doing what I want to do, Justin. I don't stay in Weaver because I'm afraid to go out into the big bad world. I stay because this is my home. Because every…everything I love is here. You used to understand that. I thought you did, anyway."

"If this is still about what happened four years ago—"

"It's not. What you want out of life has always been different than what I want out of life. When we were kids it didn't matter. But we're not kids anymore. I'm not the kind of girl who can do the friends-with-benefits thing. That might be fine for someone else, but it's just not in my genetic makeup, I guess. I still believe sex should mean more than that. And now that we've gone *there*—" she waved her hand "—I don't know how to get back to just being friends again. Either I get mad. Or you get mad. And someone inevitably notices. You're going to be here for another few weeks, so if only for the sake of a little sanity and keeping our families from getting needlessly upset, I think it would be best if we keep our distance from each other. At least when we have a choice about it."

"What if I don't agree?"

She lifted her shoulder. "Give me a better solution."

He stared at her. Unfortunately, he didn't have one.

So when she broke the tense silence between them by getting in her car, he didn't stop her.

Instead, he watched the taillights of her old car until they were no longer in sight.

Chapter Twelve

"Tabby!" Hayley Banyon, looking elegantly beautiful in a royal blue gown, caught Tabby's hands and leaned forward to kiss her cheek. "I'm so glad to see you." Then she looked up at Bubba. "My goodness, Bubba. Look at you."

Tabby's cook grimaced. He was clean shaven— something she wasn't sure she'd ever seen before. He looked as though he already wanted to rip off his black bow tie, even though they'd just arrived at the party. "Feel like a trussed-up penguin," he said, tugging at his black tuxedo jacket.

"You don't look like a penguin," Hayley assured him. "You're downright handsome."

Which was a compliment that only made Bubba look even more uncomfortable. He muttered a gruff "thank you" that made Hayley's smile widen. She squeezed Tabby's hands once again before excusing herself to greet more people as they entered the high-ceilinged, marble-floored foyer.

Come with me.

Tabby shook the memory of Justin's words out of her

head and slid her hand around Bubba's arm, urging him past the beautifully decorated Christmas tree situated in the center of the spacious entry. She wanted to be there about as much as she wanted holes drilled in her head.

But she wasn't going to let Bubba down just because Justin Clay once again had her twisted in knots. *Come with me.* Just like that. Drop everything that mattered in her life to go with him simply because he'd discovered having sex with her wasn't so bad, after all.

"The sooner Vivian sees you here, the sooner you can leave," she said under her breath.

Bubba made a face. "I never wore stuff like this before."

"I've never worn an evening gown, either," Tabby said, brushing her hand down the heavy red fabric of her dress. "I'll be lucky if I don't trip over the thing and fall on my face. The only floor-length thing I've ever worn was a flannel nightgown when I was little."

As she'd hoped, Bubba's expression lightened up a little. "You don't have on your cowboy boots underneath there, do you?"

"I wish." She lifted the hem a few inches off the floor to reveal the high-heeled pumps her mother had loaned her to go with the dress. "It's going to take alcohol to make me forget the way these shoes are pinching my toes." Though why it might work for her aching toes when it didn't work to help her forget those three little words—*come with me*—she couldn't imagine.

"Pretty sure there'll be plenty of alcohol," Bubba said as they entered a living area that made even Hope and Tristan Clay's great room look small. "I've seen the boxes of stuff Montrose has been getting."

Despite herself, she realized she was gaping at the sight of the room around them, and she made herself stop.

She'd never seen so many pieces of gold furniture in one place before. But then, she'd also never seen people she'd known all of her life dressed in this much formal wear before, either. Not even at the hospital fund-raiser.

She blinked a little at the sight of Tristan Clay, decked out in a tux just as black as Bubba's. But Justin's dad wore his with enviable ease. Probably because he owned and operated the hugely successful Cee-Vid and was more accustomed to such ostentatious displays. Hope, who was standing beside her husband, looked positively radiant in a deep purple gown. They seemed deep in conversation with a couple Tabby didn't know who were similarly attired.

Even though she knew her mom had been glad for a legitimate excuse to miss the party, she was sorry that Jolie wasn't there to see all the glamour.

Right here in Weaver.

For the first time in days, the matter of Justin Clay edged slightly to one side in her mind.

"Bubba," she murmured. "I don't think we're in Kansas anymore."

He responded by turning her slightly so she could see the hostess where she was standing by a tall window, talking with a stern-looking man.

Tabby had only seen Vivian in person a few times. She figured Hayley's grandmother was probably in her eighties. But there was nothing exactly elderly about the white-haired woman. Even though Tabby's mother had described the gown she'd made for Vivian, she still blinked a little at the sight of it. Yards of white satin ought to have overwhelmed the diminutive woman, but they didn't. The shining gold fabric tied around her waist in an oversize bow ought to have seemed silly, but it didn't. Plus it matched the fancy little bolero jacket she wore.

"Do you think she planned it so she'd match the gold flecks in the upholstery?"

Fortunately, Bubba's guffaw was drowned out by Christmas music and conversation. "Knowing her, she might have." Evidently losing interest, he gestured toward a table that was set up as a bar. "Alcohol's over there."

Tabby gratefully headed over with him. This whole thing was feeling decidedly surreal, and fortification would be necessary if and when Justin got there. She'd been praying for two solid days that he'd get so involved with his work that he'd forget all about the party.

But if her prayers of the cowardly variety were answered on a regular basis, he would've gone back to Boston after Thanksgiving the way he usually did.

Gathering her wits about her, she glanced at the elaborate display spread out on the white-and-gold cloth covering the table. There was nothing as simple as beer on offer, which was one more indication that Hayley's grandmother expected those around her to adjust to her style, rather than the other way around.

What else could explain a woman who drove a Rolls-Royce around Weaver when a pickup or SUV would have been far more sensible?

Bubba seemed to take it more in stride, but then he had more personal experience with their hostess than Tabby. He simply poured himself a healthy measure of whiskey and muttered something about needing some fresh air. Tabby let him go. He was more familiar with the big new house than she was, after all.

She studied the collection of wine bottles for a moment, then chose a pinot noir. She took one sip and groaned a little.

"Something wrong with the wine?"

Startled, she glanced up at the tall man who'd stepped behind the table. "Not at all." She smiled ruefully. "It's too good. I'm afraid the usual stuff I drink is never going to satisfy me now."

"My grandmother has good taste in liquor and wine. But—" he angled his blond head and smiled "—I wish she didn't think beer was beneath her." His eyes glinted. "I might survive the evening, though, if you'll tell me that you and I aren't related."

"Mrs. Templeton is your grandmother?"

He glanced over at their hostess, who now seemed to be in heated discussion with her companion. "Yes. And that guy she's arguing with is my old man." He looked back at Tabby and stuck his hand over the bottles. "Archer Templeton."

Tabby's smile widened as she shook his hand. "You're Hayley's brother. The lawyer, right?"

"Guilty."

"She's mentioned you a few times. I'm Tabby Taggart. And I'll admit to knowing quite a few of the people here, but I'm definitely not related to any of them." Never would be.

Come with me. As what?

Archer didn't immediately release her hand. "The evening is looking up."

She flushed a little. It was hard not to. The man was crazy handsome and possessed a devilish smile. If she didn't already know the futility of it, she might have wondered if he was rocket worthy.

She slipped her hand away from his and tucked her hair behind one ear. "Do you live in Braden, Archer?"

"Sort of. I have a house there." He dropped a few ice cubes into a glass and splashed vodka over them before tossing in a few olives. "I spend more of my time in Cheyenne. Sometimes Denver." He lifted his drink. "My dad's idea of a martini." He squinted a little as he took a sip. "So if you're not one of our newfound kin, are you here with one? Hayley says our granny was choosy with her invites."

"I'm here with Bub—er, Robert Bumble." The name obviously meant nothing to him. "He cooks for your grandmother when Montrose is off."

"Ah." Archer nodded his head. "And is it serious between you and 'Bub—er, Robert'?"

She couldn't help but smile. "I would be lost without him," she said seriously, then chuckled when Archer frowned. "We actually work together," she admitted. "I run a diner here in Weaver. He's our regular cook. And I honestly couldn't do it without him."

"Well, then." His frown disappeared, and he held up his highball glass between them. "To new friends."

She narrowed her eyes at him. "Something tells me you already have a lot of *friends*, Archer."

His smile deepened. "I'll plead the Fifth on that."

She laughed and tapped the side of her wineglass against his. "To new friends."

Entering the room on Erik and Izzy's heels, Justin immediately spotted Tabby. It was hard not to. Just as she had at the hospital fund-raiser, she stood out like a shining beacon. Only tonight, instead of a shimmery white dress that stopped midthigh, she was wrapped in red from neck to toe. The only things left bare were her sleekly muscled shoulders and arms. She'd done something to her hair, too. It was as shiny as ever, but it was straight and smooth as glass, streaming behind her back.

She was Tabby. Yet she wasn't.

He was vaguely aware of Erik saying something, and then his brother and sister-in-law were crossing the fancy room, leaving him behind.

He watched Tabby and a strange man share a toast and a smile that looked way too friendly and felt his fists curl.

Without conscious thought, he moved over to them and put his arm around her. When she jumped, he merely cupped his palm around her shoulder, holding her still. "How's the wine?"

The look she gave him spoke volumes.

It didn't stop him from sliding the glass right out of her fingers. He absently did the ritual wine-tasting bit he'd perfected because of CNJ. Swirl. Sniff. Sip. He'd done it with heads of corporations and medical institutions. But he didn't take his eyes off the other man, who was giving him an assessing look in return.

"Not bad," he said, taking a longer sip. "Who's your new friend, Tab?"

She was rigid beside him. "Your cousin, actually," she said through her teeth. "Dr. Justin Clay, meet Archer Templeton." She turned away from him with a sharp little jerk that dislodged his hand. "It's been very nice meeting you, Archer. But if you'll excuse me, I'm going to go find my date." She walked away.

Both men watched her, though Archer was the one

to break his stare first. "Doctor," he drawled. "Hayley gave me the rundown, but I didn't pay her much attention. My uncle is a pediatrician."

"Not that kind of doctor. Tabby just likes jerking my chain."

"Hmm." Archer looked amused and belatedly stuck out his hand. "Which one of Squire Clay's sons do you belong to?"

Justin was supposed to be a civilized man. He crushed the appealing notion of dragging Tabby away where she'd be out of reach of guys like Archer and reluctantly shook the other man's hand. "Tristan is my father. I'm his youngest. He's Squire's youngest. And you? Where do you fit?"

Archer jerked his chin toward a white-haired lady wearing a set expression. "That gray-haired guy arguing with Granny Vivian? He's my father, Carter. Also her youngest."

Erik had reiterated the history for Justin before they'd entered the palatial house. "Your grandfather and my grandfather's first wife were brother and sister."

"Half brother and sister. But, yeah. My grandfather never knew about her, though, until they were adults."

"Your grandfather died when he was still a young man." Erik had told him that, too.

Archer nodded. "And your grandmother died while she was still a young woman." He glanced again at his grandmother. "Viv managed to piss off a lot of people in her day, including your grandfather. Otherwise, we might have learned about each other long before now. But she's trying to make up for it."

"Someone should tell her that dropping a pile of money on the hospital isn't going to sway my grandfather. Squire makes up his mind about something, it's not likely to change. Before my dad was even born, your grandmother disrespected Squire's wife because she was illegitimate. Obviously she didn't have a problem with your grandfather—she named my uncle after him. But my grandfather won't ever forget."

Archer shrugged. "I only met her earlier this year myself, but I already know that Vivian doesn't change her mind, either. Even if she has to build a brand-new fence around the obstacle of your grandfather, she's going to keep mending the rest of them. Trying to, at least. I can give her credit for that, even though my father won't."

"Seems our families have even more in common," Justin said. "Stubborn-as-hell grandparents."

"And similar taste in women." Archer's gaze traveled past Justin, obviously watching Tabby again.

Forget civilized. "She's off the market," he said flatly.

The other man's eyebrows rose. "She didn't give me that impression."

"Regardless. Look somewhere else."

Archer eyed him for a moment. Then he shrugged and topped off his glass with a shot of vodka. "Glad to meet you, Doc. I think we all might be in for an interesting evening," he added as he walked away.

Justin doubted it. If he hadn't heard from three different people that week that Tabby was going to be there with Bubba, he would have excused himself from going altogether, no matter what he'd promised his mother. He still had work to do, and the deadline was looming larger with every passing day.

But he was glad he was there. Archer Templeton was a player. Justin recognized the type.

And there was no way the guy was going to play with Tabby.

Since she'd scraped away his suggestion about Boston the way he'd scraped dog crap from his shoe, he hadn't seen or spoken with her. Until tonight.

From the corner of his eye, he saw her hugging Izzy. Physically, the two women couldn't have been more different. Izzy was short and curvaceous with white-blond hair. Tabby was tall and lean with brown hair so dark it was almost black.

But for a moment—a moment that had his hair standing on end—he imagined Tabby with a baby bump like the one Izzy sported.

He abruptly set down the whiskey he'd been about to pour into a glass and reached instead for one of the fancy-looking bottles of water. It was the same brand that Gillian used to request whenever they'd gone out. He removed the pretentious cork top and took a long drink. As it always had before, the stupidly expensive stuff tasted no better than the tap water he'd grown up with.

His parents waylaid him before he could head Tabby's way again, and he found himself enduring more Templeton introductions. So many, in fact, that he started regretting the water-over-whiskey choice. Then his aunt Rebecca and uncle Sawyer arrived, and she wanted to know how his space was working at the lab. He was in the middle of that conversation when a streak of red entered his line of sight.

"How *dare* you," Tabby said, shoving his shoulder hard. "I'm *off the market*?" Her voice rose above the music and conversation, which dwindled to nothing in the wake of her furious words.

"Calm down. You're overreacting."

Her expression grew even angrier. "*You* are the biggest jerk I have ever known. Why I ever thought I—" She pressed her lips together, breathing hard. "You know what?" She waved her hand. "I'm done. I'm just done. Weaver obviously isn't large enough for the two of us. I thought I could stick it out until you go back to Boston, but I was wrong." She turned away so sharply that her hair spun out from her shoulders.

Not caring about the shocked attention they were getting, he grabbed her arm, halting her progress. "What do you mean, you're *done*?"

She yanked out of his grip. Tears glittered in her eyes. "I mean I don't want anything to do with you! I want you out of my triplex and out of my life."

Panic slid through his gut. "That's never gonna happen. Ruby's—"

She pushed her shaking hands through her hair, raking it back from her face. "Forget Ruby's! I want no part of it as long as you're part of that equation. I *quit*!"

Chapter Thirteen

"I warned everyone that no good would come outta that woman's Christmas party last night." Justin's grandfather sat down across from him at the big round table in the Double-C's kitchen. "But nobody wants to listen to an old man anymore."

Gloria snorted softly. "Don't try the poor-me tack, Squire. Nobody buys it." She set a pitcher of syrup on the table next to the waffle she'd already given Justin. A waffle he didn't want, but one he didn't have the heart to deny.

Not when his grandmother and grandfather were the only ones who hadn't basically slammed a door in his face.

His parents were furious.

His brother was livid.

The rest of the family had pretty much been disgusted. His uncle Matt—who ran the ranch and along with his wife lived in the big house with Squire and Gloria—had blandly suggested Justin bed down in the barn. He hadn't been joking.

The howling puppy Justin had been trying to con-

tain had received a better welcome. Jaimie had grabbed
Beastie and disappeared upstairs with her, crooning
softly.

Gloria had intervened on Justin's behalf, though, ush-
ering him personally down to the basement and one of
the guest rooms there.

"Vivian didn't do a thing," his grandmother went on,
taking the seat next to Justin.

"How do you know?" Squire demanded testily. "You
weren't there."

"Only because I didn't want you to work yourself
into a heart attack if I went," she countered mildly.
"I've gotten enough accounts from everyone to feel like
I was. Get off your high horse, dear. This isn't about
Vivian. It's about Justin."

"And Tabby." His grandfather's gaze pierced through
him. "I've always had a soft spot for that little filly.
What the hell did you do to her?"

Justin pushed aside his untouched plate. He didn't
even want to have breakfast with himself. Was it any
wonder Matt and Jaimie had avoided him, too? Not even
Beastie had found her way to his lap.

"Squire," Gloria chided softly. "Barking won't solve
anything." She covered Justin's clenched fist with her
cool palm. "I'm sure everything will work out."

"Yeah," Justin muttered. "Once I haul my ass back
to Boston. Sorry, Grandma."

She looked vaguely amused. "I've certainly heard
worse. And from all accounts, you behaved like an ass
last night. Fortunately, I have plenty of practice loving
people who do that." She slid her gaze to her husband
as she squeezed Justin's fist with one hand and moved

the plate back in front of him with her other. "But not eating won't help, either."

"Only you have the gift of making me feel chastised and cherished all at the same time."

Squire thumped the end of his walking stick against the wood floor. "That's why I married her, boy." He grinned at his own humor and actually winked at Gloria.

Justin scrubbed his hands down his face. "None of this would've happened if she'd have just come to Boston with me," he muttered. He dropped his hands and stabbed his fork into the waffle, then realized that his grandparents were staring at him.

Gloria leaned toward him. "You asked Tabby to go to Boston?"

He set down the fork again. "For all the good it did. She turned me down. Flat. Cares more about the diner and Weaver than she does anything else." He caught the look the two of them exchanged. "She was pretty clear," he said in self-defense.

"But she quit managing the diner." Gloria sat back. "In front of close to fifty people, it sounds like."

"She doesn't mean it."

Neither Gloria nor Squire looked convinced.

"She doesn't." Justin's tone was confident, but only because it stemmed from something that felt uncomfortably like desperation churning inside him. "Tomorrow morning comes around, she'll be serving up those cinnamon rolls of hers at Ruby's just like usual."

She wasn't.

The diner *did* open.

Bubba had seen to that, according to Erik, who came

by the hospital Monday afternoon to lay into Justin again about the whole thing.

But Tabby had never shown. Bubba had assured Erik that she wasn't going to, either, and had grimly produced the keys to the restaurant that Tabby's brother had dropped off.

"What the hell went on between you, anyway?" Justin's brother filled the doorway of the office he was using.

He shut the laptop and the damned report he was trying and failing to write. "Nothing that's anyone else's business."

Erik gave him a look. "This is Weaver. You don't want other people in your business, you shouldn't be having scenes like you did the other night at that party."

"Did you come here to offer any helpful advice or just to bust my chops some more?"

His brother's expression darkened. "Dammit, Justin. This isn't a joke."

He stood so fast that the rolling stool he'd been using bounced off the wall and tipped onto its side. "You think I don't know that?" He got into his brother's face, staring him straight in the eye. "This is my *life*, Erik. When have you ever known me not to take that pretty freaking seriously?"

They were the same height, but his brother outweighed him by a good thirty pounds. Erik had always been patient. Peaceful. It was Justin who'd been an instigator, always trying to take down his older, brawnier brother. There'd been few times in their childhood when Erik hadn't been able to flatten Justin just from his sheer strength. Until Justin had gotten smarter. Wilier. Used his brains against his brother's brawn. Stopped trying to measure up in an area where he never could and started focusing on his own strengths. His own dreams.

Tabby had been the one to help him realize that.

His anger oozed out of him.

What was left was weariness.

He turned away from Erik, righted the stool and sat down on it. "She hates me."

Erik glanced behind him at the hospital lab, then stepped into the office and closed the door. There wasn't another seat, and he leaned back against the door, folding his arms over his chest and the visitor ID tag he was wearing. "Despite the somewhat overwhelming evidence, I kind of doubt it."

"I never should've slept with her."

Erik's eyes sharpened. "So that's it." Then he smiled faintly and shook his head. "I always wondered. The two of you were as close as Frick and Frack when we were kids. Even when you left for college and took up with Nosebleed. So what's the problem?"

"She won't come to Boston."

Erik's eyebrows shot up. "You asked Tabby to marry you?"

"*What*? No!" Justin shoved off the stool again. The office was suddenly too claustrophobic with the door closed, but he didn't want to open it and chance even more people overhearing his business.

"Well, what *did* you say?"

"I asked her to come! I got a 'thanks, but no thanks' in return."

Erik rubbed his hand over his face, looking as though he was trying not to laugh.

It annoyed Justin as much now as it had when they were kids. "Glad I'm entertaining you, bro."

Erik dropped his hand. "For a guy who runs circles around me in the brains department, you are an idiot."

"Once again. Helpful."

"Jesus, Justin. This isn't rocket science or the cure to cancer. Are you in love with Tabby or not?"

"What good does it do me if I am?"

His brother's eyes were laughing. "You've got fifty square feet in here, genius. Don't need to yell."

"I should've poisoned you with my chemistry set when we were kids."

"I'd have seen you coming and just dumped you in the water trough." Erik shook his head again and wrapped his arm around Justin's neck in a hug disguised as a choke hold. "You're a damn idiot, but you're my brother and I love you. So I'm gonna help you even though I came here to kick your butt."

He released the choke hold and pushed Justin toward the stool. "When you asked Tabby—and when I say *asked*, I'm playing fast and loose with the term— did you happen to mention the way you feel about her? I might not have a bunch of university diplomas on my walls, but I have learned a thing or two about women. And one is that you have to say the words!"

The spot between Justin's shoulder blades itched. "Tabby knows me better than anybody."

"Really?" Erik leaned back against the door again. "And I'll bet you think you know her just as well." He spread his arms. "How's that working out for you?"

Justin pushed open his laptop again. "I'll get her back to the diner."

Erik swore. "If you think this is about the diner, you

are even more dimwitted than I thought. And maybe you do deserve Nosebleed." He yanked open the office door. "Fix it, Justin. Not for me. Not for Mom and Dad. Fix it for you. And for her." Then he stepped out of the office and slammed the door.

"Tabby." Jolie followed her from the bedroom back out to the living room. She'd shown up as soon as she heard Evan had dropped off Tabby's keys with Bubba. "I know you're upset. But that diner means everything to you. Are you sure you don't want to reconsider quitting?"

Tabby set the cellophane tape she'd just retrieved on the coffee table and sat down on the floor. The only Christmas gifts she'd managed to get so far were for her nieces and nephew. At least she'd bought them before she'd quit her job. "I'm sure." She unrolled the wrapping paper.

Her mom sat on the couch beside her, setting her hand on Tabby's shoulder. "Honey."

Tabby blinked away the moisture that glazed her vision. "I'm fine."

Jolie sighed and moved her hand away. "I should have seen what was going on between you and Justin."

"Why?" She sniffed and tore off a piece of tape, securing the festive red-and-green paper in place. "Not even Justin can see it." She snapped off another piece. "Of course he's an impossible male," she added darkly.

"They all are at one time or another," Jolie replied. "Even your father. It's in their genetic code, I think. Just as being an impossible female at one time or another is in ours."

Tabby's lips twisted. "Fair-minded as always."

"Have you, ah, spoken with him since—"

"Nope. No reason to. We've said more than enough."

"Hope told me he's staying at the Double-C."

Her hands faltered for a moment. "Good place for Beastie," she said. And Justin had always had a soft spot for his grandmother. And Gloria for him.

Tabby folded the ends of the paper, taped them down and finally pushed aside the wrapped box. "I'm not going to stay at your house on Christmas Eve this year. I'll, uh, I'll come over on Christmas Day instead."

"I'm not losing your company on Christmas Eve because you're afraid of running into Justin."

"I'm not afraid," she muttered. "But I embarrassed myself in front of everyone at Vivian Templeton's party. I'd rather just—"

"Hide."

She wasn't going to deny it. "If that's how you want to put it."

"You're my daughter. If it's a choice between you and the Clays—"

"Don't." She pushed off the floor and paced around the couch. "You and Hope are like sisters. You're not going to change a tradition I've known my entire life because of this. That's exactly what I wanted to avoid!"

Her mom sighed. "Well. Christmas Eve is still five days away. We'll figure it out."

Jolie could do all the figuring she wanted. But it wouldn't change Tabby's mind.

"I'm just glad you've got income coming in from your paintings. But if you need money—"

"I'm not going to ask you for money," Tabby cut her off before she could go any further. "I'm an adult. I have savings. And I'll find another job." She pushed her fingers into her pockets so her mom couldn't see them shaking. "In fact, I have enough savings that maybe I should just open my own restaurant! It would have to be smaller than Ruby's. But with the right space, the right staff?"

Instead of looking comforted, her mother just seemed even more alarmed. "Opening a restaurant is a huge undertaking."

"Yeah, well, maybe it's time I did something huge." Besides sleeping with Justin or causing a scene in front of darn near the entire Clay family.

Jolie glanced at her watch and pushed off the couch. "I don't want to go, but I'm doing a fitting with the mayor's wife. She's throwing a New Year's Eve party for the town council." She caught Tabby's shoulders and gave her a steady look. "Don't do anything rash."

"Anything more rash than I already have, you mean?"

"Yes." She kissed Tabby's cheek. "Call me if you need me."

"I'm fine, Mom."

"Mmm." She tucked her finger under Tabby's chin. "I remember what it feels like when your heart is breaking. So you call your mother if you need her."

Tabby's eyes flooded, and she caught her mom in a fast, tight hug. "I'll always need you," she promised thickly. Then she let her go and sniffed hard. "Now go on for your appointment before we start bawling."

"Tell me what you're doing for the rest of the day."

"I'm not going to throw myself off a cliff, if that's what you're worried about." She gestured at the toys sitting on her coffee table. "I still have to finish wrapping these. And I never got around to putting up a Christmas tree here." Her throat tightened again. She hadn't needed to, because she'd already put up the tree at Ruby's. "There's a tree lot in Braden. I might drive over and get one."

"For heaven's sake. We always cut ours fresh from behind—"

"Rebecca and Sawyer's house." She shrugged. "I'd just rather buy one." She wished she hadn't even brought up the subject, which she'd only done in order to emphasize just how fine she supposedly was. "We'll see."

"If you're going to go, don't go too late. They're calling for a winter storm by tonight." Jolie looked at her watch again and muttered a soft oath.

Tabby opened the door and nudged her mom through the doorway, getting a gust of icy-cold wind in exchange. "Go. I am—ugh. I *will* be fine." She'd been getting over Justin for years now. She ought to be used to the process by now.

She waited until her mother reached her SUV parked on the street before she closed the door and leaned back against it.

Who was she kidding?

She was never going to be used to anything when it came to Justin.

She sat back down at her coffee table and finished wrapping the presents, only to realize she was missing one for Hannah. The custom storybook was still in her locker at Ruby's.

Swearing under her breath, she looked at the clock. If she hurried, she could get to the diner before it closed up for the day.

She grabbed her coat and keys and headed out. Once she was done there, she'd keep driving on to Braden.

Get that Christmas tree.

She'd be back before dark, and tonight, anyone driving by her place would see a festively lit Christmas tree through her front window.

She was going to act like everything was fine, even if it killed her.

When he started out that morning, Justin had intended on finishing at least the first rough draft of his paper before calling it quits for the day. Getting raked over the coals by Erik had been only one of his interruptions. But even if he'd had none at all, he still wouldn't have gotten anything more accomplished than the few pages of crap he'd managed to eke out.

The hospital had been issuing announcements all day about the coming storm. Nonessential personnel were sent home. Medical teams were put on alert.

After hearing the same announcement for about the tenth time and staring at the same nonsensical paragraph in his paper for just as long, he finally packed it in. He shoved his materials into his messenger bag, locked up the office and signed out of the lab.

Outside, the weather had turned to crap. The sky couldn't seem to decide if it wanted to spit out ice or rain or snow. It wasn't dark yet, but it might as well have been with the solid sky and miserable visibility.

He flipped up his collar and bent his head against the driving cold as he ran across the lot to his truck. He saw at least a half dozen other people doing the same thing and hoped they didn't have far to drive.

He cranked the engine and mentally blessed his uncle Matt, whose attention to everything on the Double-C— equipment, vehicles, stock—was as reliable as always. The cold engine started without a hitch. He let it run for several minutes until the heater kicked in. By the time it did, he was shivering from the cold.

"Couldn't wait until I go back to Boston to throw down the weather, I guess," he said to the universe at large and finally put the truck in gear. He didn't even realize he was heading toward the triplex until he turned the corner of Tabby's street, and he cursed his distraction. He noticed her gunboat of a car wasn't parked in the driveway when he used it to turn around and reverse course.

His tires slid as he turned the corner again, and he swore once more. Getting out to the Double-C in this frozen soup wasn't going to be a picnic. Trying at this point wasn't particularly anything he wanted to do, either.

Waiting out the storm somewhere was an option. Except the weather report said they were in for hours of it. Sleeping in his own bed at the triplex was out, but some of his cousins had places in town. The entire family was pissed with him, but not everyone would turn him out in a storm like this.

And if they did, he'd rent a bloody room at the Cozy Motel if he had to.

There were only a few other cars on Main Street as he stopped in front of Ruby's and pulled out his cell phone. He wasn't surprised that the service was out. The lights were still on in the diner, though. Leaving his truck running so he wouldn't lose the heat, he darted across the sidewalk to pull on the glass door. It was locked, and he banged his hand on it hard enough to raise the attention of Bubba back in the kitchen.

Only it wasn't Bubba who appeared and quickly crossed the diner to let him in. It was that one waitress whose name he kept forgetting. "Hey," he greeted, glancing at her name tag. "Paulette. Just need to use the phone." He started toward the counter and the kitchen door. "Weather's getting really bad. Do you have far to go to get home?"

"No." She shook her head, following on his heels. "I'm just over by the community church. Uh—"

He pushed through the swinging door and came to a dead stop at the sight of Tabby, stuck half inside the oven. "Have you decided to play Gretel now?"

She jerked her head out so fast she banged it on the edge of the oven. She rubbed her head, giving him a foul look, and closed the door. "I think it'll be okay for tomorrow, Paulette. But someone needs to tell the *owners* of this place that they should start planning on purchasing a new oven."

Paulette's worried gaze bounced from Tabby's face to Justin's and back again. "Um, I—"

"Paulette, you should go." He gave her a second look. "You do have a vehicle, don't you?"

The waitress nodded frantically. Eagerness oozed from her pores as she opened one of the lockers and pulled out a coat and scarf. She hadn't finished winding the scarf around her neck before she said a quick "G'bye" and left out the rear door.

The sound of the metal door slamming shut seemed to spur Tabby into action. She headed for the lockers, too, reaching into one that was already open. "I only came to get my personal belongings." She pulled out a pair of shoes and dropped them in a half-filled box sitting on the floor. A thick book and a hairbrush followed, then a ratty-looking sweater that she bunched up and shoved on top.

"You don't want to quit."

She kicked the locker door closed and picked up the box, only to set it on the stainless steel rolling table where she made her cinnamon rolls. "Au contraire." She brushed past him through the swinging door and checked the front lock while she doused the lights. Then she hit the power switch on the enormous coffee brewer and nudged on the cash register drawer to be sure it was latched.

She didn't look at him as she came back through the door he was holding for her. "I've decided to open a restaurant of my own." She sent him an insincere smile as she reached for the coat tossed over a box of paper goods.

He grunted impatiently. "You don't need to do that. Ruby's is—"

"Yours." She shoved her arms into the sleeves and flipped her hair out of the collar. It was back to normal again, full and wavy. And he knew it would feel silky and vibrant between his fingers.

"Maybe I'll even poach Bubba from you," she went on. "My rolls and his barbecue? We just might be able to put Ruby's out of business. Not that you'd mind. You never cared all that much about the place to begin with. Had bigger, better things in mind with the fancy degrees and the—"

"Shut up."

She gave him a dark look. "Don't like hearing the truth anymore?" She tsked. "You were a better man when you were ten than you are now."

"The truth?" He advanced on her. "The truth is I've got a job where I feel like the only people I'm helping are shareholders. Which means everything I've done for the past ten years has been a freaking waste of time."

Her expression didn't soften. "If you don't like what you're doing, then change it! I didn't even have to earn a doctorate to figure that one out, much less my plain-Jane online college degree. I knew being an artist wasn't for me. But running this place was."

He stopped short. "You finished your bachelor's degree? When? Why didn't you tell me?"

"A couple years ago. It wasn't that big a deal."

"You've been working here full-time since you graduated from high school. Of course it's a big deal. I know how much that mattered to you."

"Yeah, well, we weren't exactly sharing life news then." She reached for the metal door but didn't push it open. "How long have you been unhappy in your job?"

"A few years now. But like you said. We haven't been big on the whole sharing thing for a while now."

She rubbed her hand against the door latch. "Is it because of Gillian? Your job dissatisfaction, I mean."

"No. That, at least, is one thing I am certain about. Gillian and the job. No matter what anyone thought, they never went hand in hand. Not to me."

Tabby chewed her lip for a moment, then shook her head slightly. "I thought you came in to use the phone."

"I did."

"Well." She gestured at the phone hanging on the wall. "Have at it. Door here will lock automatically after you leave." She flipped up her hood and grabbed her box before pushing the door open. Sleet drove in around her.

"Tabby, wait." He crossed the kitchen in long strides and grabbed her arm, pulling her back inside and dragging the door closed again. In just those few seconds, the floor inside the doorway had gotten covered with the icy stuff. "It's not safe. Let that die down some first."

She clearly wanted to argue. But she also knew he was right. "I don't want to be here with you."

He swallowed that blow. "I know. I'm sorry."

She exhaled and pushed off her hood. Set down the box and pulled off her coat again.

Then she crossed the kitchen, giving him a wide berth, and turned on Bubba's radio. The music stuttered with static, and she twisted the dial a few times until it cleared. Without saying a word, she went through the swinging door. "You're gonna have a dead battery in that truck before long," she called back to him. "Headlights are still on."

He exhaled. He'd left the truck running. But it couldn't run forever. And if it stalled, she was right. He strode through the dim diner, unlocked the front door again and went outside. It only took a few seconds to shut off the engine and lights and return to the diner, but he still felt soaked.

She silently handed him a dry towel and then went to sit on one of the counter stools, dropping her head on her folded arms.

"You didn't use this thing to wipe the floors or toilets, did you?" As an attempt to lighten the situation, it fell pretty flat.

"Have no idea," she said, her voice muffled. "I don't work here anymore."

He ran the towel over his head, then went into the bathroom and held his hands under warm water until they didn't feel like frozen chunks.

Then he looked at himself in the ancient mirror over the plain white sink.

"Fix it," he muttered.

He dried his hands and left the bathroom. He pulled off the wet leather coat that wasn't giving him much warmth, anyway, and hung it on the coat tree by the door to dry. He checked the thermostat to make sure the heat was still running.

She hadn't moved but was still sitting there, hunched over the counter, her head on her arms, dark hair spreading over her slender shoulders.

"You were right," he said.

Chapter Fourteen

Tabby wished she could block out the sound of Justin's voice. She wished she hadn't stopped at the diner to pick up Hannah's gift. If she hadn't, she wouldn't have gotten hung up balancing the till for Paulette and then fiddling with the finicky oven. She would have been long gone before Justin came in.

Of course, she might have stupidly forged on to Braden with her prove-she-was-fine Christmas tree quest and gotten stuck out in the middle of nowhere in the storm, too.

She exhaled and straightened. "Right about what?"

"Sex should mean more than that."

She froze. Inside, though, her nerves began lashing around as violently as the sleet pounding against the windows.

"It just never did. Before."

She stared blindly at the stacks of white china on the shelves opposite her.

"Not with Gillian," he said. "Not with anyone. Even Collette, I guess, if I go back that far. It just…never did. Until you."

She clenched her teeth, feeling something hollow out inside her chest.

"You were a virgin."

She closed her eyes.

"That first time."

"It doesn't matter what I was four years ago. I said I… I forgave you." She surreptitiously swiped her cheek and cleared her throat. "And I didn't think you even noticed that."

"I noticed. I thought talking about it would've just made it worse."

She swallowed a choked laugh that held no amusement. "That logic still applies."

"I don't know why her name came out. I knew exactly who I was with. I wasn't thinking about anyone but you. I couldn't think about anyone but you. The way you felt. The way you tasted—"

"Justin, please. I can't do this."

"Why?"

Her throat felt like a vise. "Because it hurts too much," she whispered.

She heard his footsteps as he moved closer. "Why does it hurt?"

She shook her head without answering.

He stepped closer again. She couldn't see him. Didn't want to turn around and see him.

But her storming nerves imagined him standing only inches away.

"I know why I hurt." His already deep voice dropped a few more notches. "Do you want to know? Do you care? Erik—" He let out an impatient sound. "He says the words matter. God knows I've always gone out of my way to justify how different I am from him, but he's got the life he wants and I—"

She clenched the edge of the counter and pushed the revolving stool around.

He wasn't standing inches behind her.

He was still halfway across the room. But even in the dwindling, storm-drenched light from outside the windows, she could see the tight set of his face.

"And I don't," he finished.

"You don't have to justify the person you are. You're the only one who's ever believed that. Do you have any idea at all how *proud* they are of you?" She gestured toward the windows. "That whole town out there is proud of you." Tears clogged her nose. Choked her voice. "You're our...our very...own genius."

"If I was a genius, why did I take Collette to our high school prom?" He closed the distance between them and slid his hands around her face, making her look up at him, even though she tried to avoid it. "Why didn't I take *you*? Then it would have been you and me on a blanket spread out by the swimming hole making love under the stars, and it *would* have meant something." He brushed his thumbs over her wet cheeks. "It would have meant a hell of a lot of something."

"Justin—"

"I have loved you for more years than I can remember," he said gruffly. "And I've been *in* love with you for most of them."

She caught her lip in her teeth to keep in the sob. She shook her head. "No."

"Yes." He brushed his mouth over hers.

She trembled. Even though she was determined not to give in, her arms went around his neck. Her fingers slid through his thick, damp hair. "Don't tell me you didn't like having sex with Collette after prom. You crowed about it to Caleb for days."

"That's what high school guys do." He pulled her off the stool and up against him. "And high school was a long time ago." He closed his mouth over hers again. "Kiss me back, Tabitha."

She shuddered.

And kissed him back.

His hands tightened on the small of her back, dragging her even closer, and she drew away, hauling in a desperate breath. "Justin, we can't just—"

He lifted her right off her feet and pushed through the swinging door to the kitchen, where he set her down again. "No windows here."

Before she could protest—as if she had even a whispering thought of protest—he whipped her flannel shirt over her head and dropped it on the floor. "Someone could come in."

"Ruby's closes at two." He pushed aside her thin bra strap and kissed her bare shoulder. "It's well past that. And even if it weren't—" he slid her hair away and kissed the side of her neck, then her earlobe "—just listen," he whispered.

Shivers danced down her spine. The furnace was still running, but the air in the kitchen would have been cool if not for the heat of him against her. "Listen to what?" The sound of her heartbeat thudding in her head? The sound of his breath against her ear?

"The storm. Nobody is out in that."

She closed her eyes and pulled his mouth back to hers while blindly feeling down his chest for buttons to liberate. The only storm she knew was the one collecting inside her.

Justin seemed to know it, too. His kiss deepened, and his arms hardened around her for a moment before he pulled back long enough to yank off his shirt and spread it over the stainless steel rolling table. Then he was lifting her again until she was sitting on it. Bubba's radio was spewing soft static instead of music, and rain was driving against the roof.

Justin's hand slid under her thigh, running slowly down the back of her calf as he straightened her leg and finally reached her cowboy boot, tugging it off. After removing the other one, too, he pulled her gently off the table and unfastened her jeans. Peeled them away.

Then he hauled in a deep breath that roused her out of her seduced stupor.

She ran her hands over his bare, sinewy shoulders. Trailed them over the swirl of dark hair covering his hard chest, following downward as it narrowed to a fine line, beyond the round divot that was his navel, and disappeared beneath his jeans.

As many nights as she'd spent tormented by fantasies of this very thing, her fingers shook as she fumbled with his belt. His fly.

And he just smiled faintly and brushed her hands away, finishing the job himself while he settled his lips on hers again. So slowly and sweetly that she would have fallen in love with him right then and there if she hadn't already done so half a lifetime ago. And when the rest of his clothes had gone the way of hers, he set her on the table once more and pulled her thighs around his. "Tell me, Tabby," he murmured, pressing against her, so close but not close enough. "Tell me the words."

Even though Tabby knew it wouldn't last—it couldn't possibly last when Justin had always been meant for so much more than her and the small-town life that she loved—she twined her legs around him and arched, taking him in with a gasp. "I love you, Justin. I love you, I love—" His mouth swallowed the rest.

And neither one of them said any more.

There was just the hum of static. The beat of rain.

And their bodies moving in perfection.

When they finally left the diner the next morning, they emerged into a frozen world. Ice dripped from the tree branches and the picnic table behind the diner. It had collected on the doors of her car and his truck so thickly that they couldn't get either one open.

She put up a sign that Ruby's was closed because of the weather and they walked back to the triplex, she bundled in her hooded coat and Justin in a sweatshirt of Bubba's they'd purloined from his locker layered underneath the leather jacket. It wasn't perfect, but for the three blocks, it was enough to keep both of them from frostbite.

When they got inside, she immediately went to the fireplace and set a match to the wood already there while Justin turned up the furnace and started the shower. She watched until she was sure the small flame was going to take and then pulled off her boots and went down the hall to the bathroom. The sight of steam beginning to curl around the shower curtain was welcome.

The sight of Justin without a stitch on was a revelation. The man was so physically beautiful it seemed a shock each time she witnessed it.

"Guess I don't have to worry about hot water," she said faintly.

"Nope." He tugged her close and started pulling at her clothes. "Get nekkid."

She laughed softly. "Nekkid?"

His violet eyes were wicked. "It's more fun than naked." He kissed her nose and lightly slapped her butt, then stepped into the shower. "Oh, yeah."

She pressed her hand to her chest and felt her uneven heartbeat. *Oh, yeah.*

Then she blew out a breath and quickly finished shedding her clothes. "You never called the Double-C last night."

"They'll have figured out I was at the diner. Truck's still parked in plain sight right in front of it. Sheriff's department had cruisers out. Word will have gotten back."

"I hope Beastie's okay."

He laughed. "That dog is getting better treatment than I am." He snaked an arm out from the shower curtain and yanked her under the water with him.

She laughed, too, then sputtered when she got a mouthful of hot water. "I still have on my socks!"

"Makes you all the more nekkid," he assured her and pulled her close.

Later, when the water was running cold and the bathroom floor was drenched from the splashing, she had to admit it.

Nekkid was more fun than naked.

The sun came out of the clouds that afternoon and the frozen world turned into a constantly dripping one.

Justin called the Double-C to let them know he was back at the triplex. His grandmother wryly told him that she already knew. Mrs. Wachowski had said as much to the church deacon who'd called to check in on her after the storm, and the deacon had passed it on to her daughter who housecleaned a few times a month for Hope Clay.

"And so on and so forth," Justin said after he hung up. "Life in Weaver, where everyone knows what everyone else is doing."

Tabby chewed the inside of her cheek and finished adding the dishes from their lunch to the dishwasher. "I suppose we should go back to the diner. See if the vehicles have thawed out, too."

He nodded and prowled to the front window, looking out. "At the very least I need to get my research stuff."

"For the paper you're writing." She looked away from the long line of his back, sharply outlined by the white shirt he'd been wearing since the afternoon before. "Are you close to being finished?"

His snort said it all.

She slowly shut the dishwasher door and dried her hands on a towel. "Did you decide the data was accurate at least?"

"It's accurate." He turned away from the window. "I think Mrs. Wachowski and Mr. Rowe are getting busy."

She blinked. "I…what? He's fifteen years younger than her!"

"Yeah, well." His lips tilted in a smile. "The heart wants what it wants and all that."

How well she knew it.

"You're imagining things."

"He just left her place wearing a pink flannel robe over his boxers."

She clapped her hand over her eyes as if she could

rid the image from her mind. "Oh, good grief. Don't tell me that."

Justin chuckled as he went down the hall. She thought he was going into her bedroom, but when she followed, she found him in her studio, looking through the paintings that she hadn't yet decided were good enough to give to Bolieux.

"You sent off that blizzardy-looking one, didn't you."

"Yes."

"I liked it."

"So did I. I think it was one of my better efforts." She didn't want to think about the painting or the sentiment that had inspired it. But she did know she was going to do everything she could to get it back. "I'll grab my coat and we can head out. If you're ready."

He straightened. "I am."

Less than a half hour later, they were back at the diner. It was as quiet as it had been when they left it.

"I think I'm going to stay," she said after Justin had successfully gotten into his truck and pulled out his bulging bag. "If I know you, you'll be working on that stuff the rest of the day, anyway. I might as well be useful here. Get a jump on things for tomorrow."

"Unquitting?"

She pressed her teeth together in a crooked smile. Apparently, she could no more stick to her resolution about Ruby's than get over Justin. "So it would seem."

"Good." He kissed her thoroughly, then hitched the bag over his shoulder. "I'll walk over to the hospital," he told her. "Easier than driving on ice. Call me when you're finished."

She nodded and watched until he disappeared around the corner. Then she sighed a little and went back inside the diner. No matter what had occurred between her and Justin over the past twenty-four hours, they were still the same people they'd always been.

She turned on Bubba's radio, found a station playing Christmas music without too much static and pulled on an apron.

She was crazy in love with a man who would probably never stay. Which meant there was only one thing to do.

Start another batch of dough. Same as she'd done day in and day out for years.

The lull lasted five days.

Five perfect days of Justin working at the hospital lab, and filling her nights with passion and laughter, and more than a few arguments when it came to the television remote control and whose turn it was to take Beastie out to do her business.

Five perfect days that came to a screeching halt the day before Christmas when Tabby got home from a quick run to Classic Charms only to find a painfully familiar blonde woman hanging around outside the triplex.

Even though the desire to keep driving was strong, Tabby pulled into the driveway and parked. She clipped Beastie's leash on the puppy's collar. "Come on, sweetie." She slowly pushed open the car door and climbed out of the car.

The ice from the winter storm had all melted. So had most of the snow. After Beastie hopped down from the car, she trotted over to a corner of dead grass and squatted, staring up at Tabby for approval. "Good girl," she murmured and pushed her car door closed.

She didn't speak as Gillian headed toward her, the

high heels of her tall black boots clicking on the sidewalk. She had on camel-colored pants tucked into her boots and a clinging ivory turtleneck beneath a long black leather coat that looked expensive as hell. She made Tabby, dressed in checked flannel and jeans, feel like a bumpkin.

"I remember you," the other woman greeted. "You were at that quaint little diner when I came looking for my fiancé. It appeared to be out of business when I drove by there today."

Tabby's neck stiffened. "Not out of business at all," she said. "Just closed for the holiday. What are you doing here, Gillian?"

Gillian pushed her blond hair behind her shoulder, looking pleased. "I guess Justin told you all about me."

Bat-crap crazy, Tabby thought. She didn't voice it.

"He's working at the hospital." He was finally making headway with his research paper and expected to finish it today. Then in the evening, they were heading to her parents' place to spend Christmas Eve with their families.

But Gillian shook her head. "I've been to the hospital. He wasn't there. They told me he'd left several hours ago."

Tabby ignored the uneasy surprise that niggled at her belly. There could be a dozen reasons to explain Justin's whereabouts. Just because he'd very specifically told her he'd be busy there the entire day was no cause for concern. "I can leave him a message if you like."

Gillian rolled her eyes, dismissing the offer. "I'll wait." She smiled confidently. "He'll want to see me. I came all this way, after all." She gestured toward Mrs.

Wachowski's window. "The old woman told me you own the building."

Tabby knew her neighbor was watching behind the twitching curtains. "Yes."

"Perfect. You can let me into his apartment."

"Is Justin expecting you?"

Gillian laughed lightly. "No. But he loves my little surprises. He's going to be so glad I made it for Christmas Eve. We always spend that together, no matter what's going on in our lives. It's kind of our own special time. I'm sure you understand." She held out her hand. "And I'll take our dog. Nice of you to watch her for us while Justin's busy. I hope he's paying you for it."

The niggling gained little claws that scratched from the inside. Justin hadn't been home to Weaver for Christmas in years. Before Tabby's imagination could start running riot, she handed over Beastie's leash. If nothing else, she found satisfaction in the puppy's total lack of interest in Gillian.

"So, the key?" Gillian rubbed her bare hands together. "I don't want to be an ice cube when Justin arrives."

"Sure," Tabby said, abruptly deciding that letting Gillian into the end unit was better than inviting her into her own. The other woman couldn't do any harm. There weren't even very many pieces of Justin's clothing left over there. "I'll get the key."

She unlocked her door and went inside, closing it after her, just in case Gillian got the idea of following her. She knew it was probably rude leaving her outside on the sidewalk, but she didn't care.

She called Justin's cell phone as she retrieved the spare key. Not only did he not answer, but the call went straight to his voice mail. That was typical when he was working.

But if he wasn't at the hospital, he wasn't exactly working.

"Call me when you can," she said after the beep, and hung up.

She looked at herself in the dresser mirror and abruptly grabbed her hairbrush, yanking it through her disorderly hair. Then, annoyed with herself, she tossed the brush down again, grabbed the spare key and stomped outside.

The sight of Gillian in Justin's arms punched the breath out of her.

She must have made some noise, some animal sound of distress, because Beastie bolted toward her, yanking the chain out of Gillian's grasp. The puppy shot across the sidewalk, chain dragging behind her, and vaulted into Tabby's arms.

"I knew it," she told Justin over the dog's head. "She's not out of your life."

At the sound of Tabby's wounded voice, Justin finished impatiently yanking Gillian's arms from around his neck and pushed her away. She'd launched herself at him so fast he hadn't been able to evade her. "Yes, she is," he told Tabby firmly.

Then he looked back at Gillian. "What the hell are you doing here?"

She huffed. "We spend Christmas together. We always spend Christmas together."

"*We* aren't a *we*."

"Of course we are," Gillian returned. In her typically self-involved way, she wasn't fazed at all by his cold welcome. "You're getting the promotion, by the way. Daddy told me just yesterday."

"I know I am." He looked toward Tabby where she was standing like a statue on her porch. "He called me this morning." Charles had said he wasn't waiting on the research paper. He'd made up his mind and wanted to make the announcement official before the end of the year.

And Justin had spent the rest of the morning deciding what to do about it.

"Congratulations," Tabby said. Her eyes were dark as she studied him over Beastie's silky head.

"I got a promotion, too," Gillian added.

"Your father told me." He was aware of the look she was sliding between him and Tabby.

"So you know that if I say so, *your* promotion turns to dust. Just like that." She snapped her fingers.

"I already turned it down."

He was sure the only time in the history of the world when Tabby and Gillian would think alike was that moment, when they said, *"What?"* in unison.

He ignored Gillian and focused on Tabby.

"I turned down the promotion," he said, slowly heading toward her. "In fact, I turned everything down." Aside from admitting to Tabby that he loved her, it had been one of the most freeing moments he'd ever known. "I told him I'd finish the paper. But I'm not going back."

Gillian grabbed him from behind. "Have you lost your mind?"

He shook her off. "Gillian, you don't really want me. You just don't like losing."

Her eyebrows skyrocketed. "Losing." She looked from him to Tabby. "I suppose you mean to *her*?"

He gained a visceral, abrupt understanding of Squire's continued hatred of Vivian Templeton for once snubbing his wife.

"I can be polite," he warned softly, "but wipe that sneer off your face when you look at the woman I love, or I'll do it for you."

She gaped. "You wouldn't dare."

"He wouldn't," Tabby said suddenly. She stepped off the porch and let Beastie down as she approached. Color rode her cheeks, and her dark eyes snapped. She looked like a dark-haired Valkyrie set on attack. "But I would."

"My father's never going to stand for this," Gillian warned Justin, even though she took a wary step back from Tabby.

He almost smiled at the sight of it.

"Get off my property," Tabby told her.

Gillian rolled her eyes. "People like you don't tell people like me what to do."

He saw Tabby's fist clench and caught it midair. She shot him a look, and his smile did break free. "You don't know what kind of damage I just saved you from," he told Gillian. He kissed Tabby's knuckles. "She packs a punch. Always has."

"Don't talk about me like I'm not here," Tabby said, looking as if she still wanted to break Gillian's plastic surgery–perfect nose.

He firmly peeled open her fist. Turned her palm upward and kissed it. "There's a better use for your hand," he said. He pulled the small ring box out of his pocket and set it on her palm. He'd searched all three jewelry stores in Braden that day before finding the perfect one.

Her eyes widened. Her lips parted. "What, uh, what is that?"

"You know what it is." He opened the box. The diamond ring nestled on the velvet inside sparkled in the winter sunlight. "It's our future."

She moistened her lips. Her eyes suddenly shimmered.

"Marry me, Tabby." He offered a crooked smile. "You might have to give me a job down at the diner for a while until I find gainful employment here in Weaver, but—"

"Yes," she said thickly.

Gillian made a disgusted sound. "You're an idiot, Justin Clay. You have no idea what you're turning down."

He didn't even glance at her. He was too busy sliding his ring on Tabby's trembling finger. "I'm not an idiot anymore," he said and leaned down to press his lips to hers. "I love you, Tabbers."

"I love you, too," she whispered, sliding her arms around his neck.

"I'm taking my dog," Gillian snapped and snatched up the puppy, who immediately started whining.

Tabby slid her fingers through Justin's hair and smiled into his violet eyes. Violet eyes that she'd be looking into for the rest of their lives. "She probably deserves Beastie," she murmured. "She'd love making a meal out of that leather coat Gillian's wearing."

His eyes crinkled. "Yeah. But Beastie doesn't deserve her." He snapped his fingers, and the puppy launched herself out of Gillian's arms. He scooped her up and put his other arm around Tabby again. They turned to go back into the house. "Did you finish your Christmas shopping?"

"I did." Her arm came around his waist and her head

found his shoulder. "Still in the car. I'll need to wrap it before we go to my parents. Did you really quit your job?"

"I really did." He pressed his lips against her forehead. "What time do we have to be at your folks'?"

"Little later this afternoon."

"Good." He handed Beastie to her and swept her off her feet.

She gasped, catching his shoulder with her free hand. "Justin! What are you doing?"

He laughed. "Carrying my family inside," he said and did exactly that.

Tabby glanced over his shoulder as she reached behind him to push the door closed. The only thing she saw of Gillian was the exhaust from her car as she roared away.

Tabby pushed and the door closed with a soft click. She expected him to put her down. Instead he just carried her down the hall toward the bedroom. "You're really sure about this?"

"Yup." He lowered her onto the bed and started pulling off her shirt. "Plenty of time."

She unclipped Beastie's leash and let the dog loose on the bed. The diamond ring felt strange and unfamiliar on her finger. "I mean about marrying me. About staying."

"Yup." He suddenly knelt on the floor in front of her and kissed her finger where the ring sat. "I *had* planned to wait until tonight to ask you, but when the moment strikes and all that." His eyes met hers. "Are *you* sure?"

She pressed her lips to his forehead. His cheeks. "I've been sure about you since I was fifteen years old," she whispered and brushed her lips over his.

Behind them, Beastie pawed experimentally at one of the pillows, then sank her teeth into the fabric, giving a sharp little pull. It tore, and she discovered a fantasy world of feathers that puffed out around her when she pounced. She gave a blissful yip.

Neither Tabby nor Justin even glanced her way.

Epilogue

"Happy New Year, Mrs. Clay."

Tabby wrinkled her nose against a tickle and opened her eyes to find Justin wielding a little white feather. Even after a week, they were still finding them all over the house.

She rolled toward him. "I'm not Mrs. Clay yet."

"You are in my mind." Beneath the quilt covering her bed, he swept his hand down her bare hip. "Only thing holding it up is a marriage license."

"And a wedding," she said on a chuckle that ended with a little gasp when his hand slid between her thighs. "Both—ah—both of our mothers will revolt if we don't give them that."

"So pick a date and I can stop avoiding the question when my mom calls every day asking. I think she's afraid I'll mess it up or something."

Tabby pushed his wide shoulders until he was flat on his back and slid over him. "No, she's not." She grasped his hard length and watched his eyes roll. She loved the fact that she could make him just as crazy as he made her. She balanced herself with one hand on the wall behind his head, accidentally knocking into the painting she'd recalled from Bolieux. It had arrived by messenger on Christmas Day. It had cost her a small fortune, but it was the only gift she wanted to give him. Justin had flattened her in return by giving her *his* gift—ownership of Ruby's. He and Erik had both signed the deed. She still couldn't believe they'd done it. Or that they'd refused to take it back when she argued with them that it was too much.

She moved her hand away from the wall and the painting slid back in place. "February twenty-eighth," she said, suddenly guiding him into her.

"What about it?"

"Wedding."

"Right." His fingers tightened around her hips. "Wedding. Perfect."

She exhaled shakily. "Have you decided about Rebecca's offer? The lab directorship?"

"Probably take it." He inhaled on a hiss.

"What about Charles?" His former boss hadn't taken Justin's resignation lying down. He'd come back with an offer that Justin could work wherever he wanted. As long as it was for CNJ. He'd even promised reassigning his daughter to a position in Europe—something Gillian had leaped on with glee.

"It's good to have options," Justin said and suddenly reversed their positions. "Wanna make a baby?"

She stared into his eyes, easily forgetting everything else in the world but him. "How do you know we haven't already?"

He went still. Deep inside her, she could feel the heat of him reaching to her very soul. "Trying to tell me something, Tabbers?"

She smiled slightly. "No. But we haven't exactly been careful." In fact, they'd been downright uncareful, if she wanted to put a fine point to it.

"Do you want to have a baby?"

"I want to have your babies," she whispered. She'd just never dreamed they'd ever come to be. "Beastie can't be an only child."

His smile was slow. "Well, then." He gently thumbed away the tear slipping down her cheek and lowered his mouth to hers. "Guess we'd better get to work…"

* * * * *

Don't miss these other stories in New York Times *and* USA TODAY *bestselling author Allison Leigh's long-running* RETURN TO THE DOUBLE-C *series:*

THE RANCHER'S DANCE
COURTNEY'S BABY PLAN
A WEAVER PROPOSAL
A WEAVER VOW
A WEAVER BEGINNING
A WEAVER CHRISTMAS GIFT
ONE NIGHT IN WEAVER…

Available from Harlequin.

Officer Wyn Bailey has found herself wanting more from her boss—and older brother's best friend—for a while now. Will sexy police chief Cade Emmett let his guard down long enough to embrace the love he secretly craves?

Read on for a sneak peek at the newest book in New York Times bestselling author RaeAnne Thayne's **HAVEN POINT** *series,*
RIVERBEND ROAD,
available July 2016 from HQN Books.

CHAPTER ONE

"THIS WAS YOUR dire emergency? Seriously?"

Officer Wynona Bailey leaned against her Haven Point Police Department squad car, not sure whether to laugh or pull out her hair. "That frantic phone call made it sound like you were at death's door!" she exclaimed to her great-aunt Jenny. "You mean to tell me I drove here with full lights and sirens, afraid I would stumble over you bleeding on the ground, only to find you in a standoff with a baby moose?"

The gangly-looking creature had planted himself in the middle of the driveway while he browsed from the shrubbery that bordered it. He paused in his chewing to watch the two of them out of long-lashed dark eyes.

He was actually really cute, with big ears and a curious face. She thought about pulling out her phone to take a picture that her sister could hang on the local wildlife bulletin board in her classroom but decided Jenny probably wouldn't appreciate it.

"It's not the calf I'm worried about," her great-aunt said. "It's his mama over there."

She followed her aunt's gaze and saw a female moose on the other side of the willow shrubs, watching them with much more caution than her baby was showing.

While the creature might look docile on the outside, Wyn knew from experience a thousand-pound cow could move at thirty-five miles an hour and wouldn't hesitate to take on anything she perceived as a threat to her offspring.

"I need to get into my garage, that's all," Jenny practically wailed. "If Baby Bullwinkle there would just move two feet onto the lawn, I could squeeze around him, but he won't budge for anything."

She had to ask the logical question. "Did you try honking your horn?"

Aunt Jenny glared at her, looking as fierce and stern as she used to when Wynona was late turning in an assignment in her aunt's high school history class.

"Of course I tried honking my horn! And hollering at the stupid thing and even driving right up to him, as close as I could get, which only made the mama come over to investigate. I had to back up again."

Wyn's blood ran cold, imagining the scene. That big cow could easily charge the sporty little convertible her diminutive great-aunt had bought herself on her seventy-fifth birthday.

What would make them move along? Wynona sighed, not quite sure what trick might disperse a couple of stubborn moose. Sure, she was trained in Krav Maga martial arts, but somehow none of those lessons seemed to apply in this situation.

The pair hadn't budged when she pulled up with her lights and sirens blaring in answer to her aunt's desperate phone call. Even if she could get them to move, scaring them out of Aunt Jenny's driveway would probably only migrate the problem to the neighbor's yard.

She was going to have to call in backup from the state wildlife division.

"Oh, no!" her aunt suddenly wailed. "He's starting on the honeysuckle! He's going to ruin it. Stop! Move it. Go on now." Jenny started to climb out of her car again, raising and lowering her arms like a football referee calling a touchdown.

"Aunt Jenny, get back inside your vehicle!" Wyn exclaimed.

"But the honeysuckle! Your dad planted that for me the summer before he…well, you know."

Wyn's heart gave a sharp little spasm. Yes. She *did* know. She pictured the sturdy, robust man who had once watched over his aunt, along with everybody else in town. He wouldn't have hesitated for a second here, would have known exactly how to handle the situation.

Wynnie, anytime you're up against something bigger than you, just stare 'em down. More often than not, that will do the trick.

Some days, she almost felt like he was riding shotgun next to her.

"Stay in your car, Jenny," she said again. "Just wait there while I call Idaho Fish and Game to handle things. They probably need to move them to higher ground."

"I don't have time to wait for some yahoo to load up his tranq gun and hitch up his horse trailer, then drive over from Shelter Springs! Besides that honeysuckle, which is priceless to me, I have seventy-eight dollars' worth of groceries in the trunk of my car that will be ruined if I can't get into the house. That includes four pints of Ben & Jerry's Cherry Garcia that's going to be melted red goo if I don't get it in the freezer fast—and that stuff is not exactly cheap, you know."

Her great-aunt looked at her with every expectation that she would fix the problem and Wyn sighed again. Small-town police work was mostly about problem solving—and when she happened to have been born and raised in that small town, too many people treated her like their own private security force.

"I get it. But I'm calling Fish and Game."

"You've got a piece. Can't you just fire it into the air or something?"

Yeah, unfortunately, her great-aunt—like everybody else in town—watched far too many cop dramas on TV and thought that was how things were done.

"Give me two minutes to call Fish and Game, then I'll see if I can get him to move aside enough that you can pull into your driveway. Wait in your car," she ordered for the fourth time as she kept an eye on Mama Moose. "Do not, I repeat, do *not* get out again. Promise?"

Aunt Jenny slumped back into her seat, clearly disappointed that she wasn't going to have front row seats to some kind of moose-cop shoot-out. "I suppose."

To Wyn's relief, local game warden Moose Porter—who, as far as she knew, was no relation to the current troublemakers—picked up on the first ring. She explained the situation to him and gave him the address.

"You're in luck. We just got back from relocating a female brown bear and her cub away from that campground on Dry Creek Road. I've still got the trailer hitched up."

"Thanks. I owe you."

"How about that dinner we've been talking about?" he asked.

She had not been talking about dinner. Moose had been pretty relentless in asking her out for months and she always managed to deflect. It wasn't that she didn't like the guy. He was nice and funny and good-looking in a burly, outdoorsy, flannel-shirt-and-gun-rack sort of way, but she didn't feel so much as an ember around him. Not like, well, someone else she preferred not to think about.

Maybe she would stop thinking about that *someone else* if she ever bothered to go on a date. "Sure," she said on impulse. "I'm pretty busy until after Lake Haven Days, but let's plan something in a couple of weeks. Meantime, how soon can you be here?"

"Great! I'll definitely call you. And I've got an ETA of about seven minutes now."

The obvious delight left her squirming and wishing she had deflected his invitation again.

Fish or cut line, her father would have said.

"Make it five, if you can. My great-aunt's favorite honeysuckle bush is in peril here."

"On it."

She ended the phone call just as Jenny groaned, "Oh. Not the butterfly bush, too! Shoo. Go on, move!"

While she was on the phone, the cow had moved around the shrubs nearer her calf and was nibbling on the large showy blossoms on the other side of the driveway.

Wyn thought about waiting for the game warden to handle the situation, but Jenny was counting on her. She couldn't let a couple of moose get the better of her. Wondering idly if a Kevlar vest would protect her in the event she was charged, she climbed out of her patrol vehicle and edged around to the front bumper. "Come on. Move along. That's it."

She opted to move toward the calf, figuring the cow would follow her baby. Mindful to keep the vehicle between her and the bigger animal, she waved her arms

like she was directing traffic in a big-city intersection.
"Go. Get out of here."

Something in her firm tone or maybe her rapid-fire
movements finally must have convinced the calf she
wasn't messing around this time. He paused for just
a second, then lurched through a break in the shrubs
to the other side, leaving just enough room for Great-
Aunt Jenny to squeeze past and head for her garage to
unload her groceries.

"Thank you, Wynnie. You're the best," her aunt
called. "Come by one of these Sundays for dinner. I'll
make my fried chicken and biscuits and my Better-
Than-Sex cake."

Her mouth watered and her stomach rumbled, reminding her quite forcefully that she hadn't eaten anything since her shift started that morning.

Her great-aunt's Sunday dinners were pure deca-
dence. Wyn could almost feel her arteries clog in an-
ticipation.

"I'll check my schedule."

"Thanks again."

Jenny drove her flashy little convertible into the garage and quickly closed the door behind her.

Of all things, the sudden action of the door seemed
to startle the big cow moose where all other efforts—
including a honking horn and Wyn's yelling and arm-
peddling—had failed. The moose shied away from the
activity, heading in Wyn's direction.

Crap.

Heart pounding, she managed to jump into her vehicle and yank the door closed behind her seconds before
the moose charged past her toward the calf.

The two big animals picked their way across the

lawn and settled in to nibble Jenny's pretty red-twig dogwoods.

Crisis managed—or at least her part in it—she turned around and drove back to the street just as a pickup pulling a trailer with the Idaho Fish and Game logo came into view over the hill.

She pushed the button to roll down her window and Moose did the same. Beside him sat a game warden she didn't know. Moose beamed at her and she squirmed, wishing she had shut him down again instead of giving him unrealistic expectations.

"It's a cow and her calf," she said, forcing her tone into a brisk, businesslike one and addressing both men in the vehicle. "They're now on the south side of the house."

"Thanks for running recon for us," Moose said.

"Yeah. Pretty sure we managed to save the Ben & Jerry's, so I guess my work here is done."

The warden grinned at her and she waved and pulled onto the road, leaving her window down for the sweet-smelling June breezes to float in.

She couldn't really blame a couple of moose for wandering into town for a bit of lunch. This was a beautiful time around Lake Haven, when the wildflowers were starting to bloom and the grasses were long and lush.

She loved Haven Point with all her heart, but she found it pretty sad that the near-moose encounter was the most exciting thing that had happened to her on the job in days.

Her cell phone rang just as she turned from Clover Hill Road to Lakeside Drive. She knew by the ringtone just who was on the other end and her breathing hitched a little, like always. Those stone-cold embers she had

been wondering about when it came to Moose Porter
suddenly flared to thick, crackling life.

Yeah. She knew at least one reason why she didn't
go out much.

She pushed the phone button on her vehicle's hands-
free unit. "Hey, Chief."

"Hear you had a little excitement this afternoon and
almost tangled with a couple of moose."

She heard the amusement in the voice of her boss—
and friend—and tried not to picture Cade Emmett
stretched out behind his desk, big and rangy and gorgeous, with that surprisingly sweet smile that broke
hearts all over Lake Haven County.

"News travels."

"Your great-aunt Jenny just called to inform me you
risked your life to save her Cherry Garcia and to tell me
all about how you deserve a special commendation."

"If she really thought that, why didn't she at least
give me a pint for my trouble?" she grumbled.

The police chief laughed, that rich, full laugh that
made her fingers and toes tingle like she'd just run full
tilt down Clover Hill Road with her arms outspread.

Curse the man.

"You'll have to take that up with her next time you
see her. Meantime, we just got a call about possible trespassers at that old wreck of a barn on Darwin Twitchell's horse property on Conifer Drive, just before the
turnoff for Riverbend. Would you mind checking it out
before you head back for the shift change?"

"Who called it in?"

"Darwin. Apparently somebody tripped an alarm he
set up after he got hit by our friendly local graffiti artist a few weeks back."

Leave it to the ornery old buzzard to set a trap for unsuspecting trespassers. Knowing Darwin and his contrariness, he probably installed infrared sweepers and body heat sensors, even though the ramshackle barn held absolutely nothing of value.

"The way my luck is going today, it's probably a relative to the two moose I just made friends with."

"It could be a skunk, for all I know. But Darwin made me swear I'd send an officer to check it out. Since the graffiti case is yours, I figured you'd want first dibs, just in case you have the chance to catch them red-handed. Literally."

"Gosh, thanks."

He chuckled again and the warmth of it seemed to ease through the car even through the hollow, tinny Bluetooth speakers.

"Keep me posted."

"Ten-four."

She turned her vehicle around and headed in the general direction of her own little stone house on Riverbend Road that used to belong to her grandparents.

The Redemption mountain range towered across the lake, huge and imposing. The snow that would linger in the moraines and ridges above the timberline for at least another month gleamed in the afternoon sunlight and the lake was that pure, vivid turquoise usually seen only in shallow Caribbean waters.

Her job as one of six full-time officers in the Haven Point Police Department might not always be overflowing with excitement, but she couldn't deny that her workplace surroundings were pretty gorgeous.

She spotted the first tendrils of black smoke above the treetops as she turned onto the rutted lane that wound its way through pale aspen trunks and thick pines and spruce.

Probably just a nearby farmer burning some weeds along a ditch line, she told herself, or trying to get rid of the bushy-topped invasive phragmites reeds that could encroach into any marshy areas and choke out all the native species. But something about the black curl of smoke hinted at a situation beyond a controlled burn.

Her stomach fluttered with nerves. She hated fire calls even more than the dreaded DD—domestic disturbance. At least in a domestic situation, there was some chance she could defuse the conflict. Fire was avaricious and relentless, smoke and flame and terror. She had learned that lesson on one of her first calls as a green-as-grass rookie police officer in Boise, when she was the first one on scene to a deadly house fire on a cold January morning that had killed three children in their sleep.

Wyn rounded the last bend in the road and saw, just as feared, the smoke wasn't coming from a ditch line or a controlled burn of a patch of invading plants. Instead, it twisted sinuously into the sky from the ramshackle barn on Darwin Twitchell's property.

She scanned the area for kids and couldn't see any. What she did see made her blood run cold—two small boys' bikes resting on their sides outside the barn.

Where there were bikes, there were usually boys to ride them.

She parked her vehicle and shoved open her door. "Hello? Anybody here?" she called.

She strained her ears but could hear nothing above the crackle of flames. Heat and flames poured off the building.

She pressed the button on the radio at her shoulder to call dispatch. "I've got a structure fire, an old barn on Darwin Twitchell's property on Conifer Drive, just before Riverbend Road. The upper part seems to be fully engulfed and there's a possibility of civilians inside, juveniles. I've got bikes here but no kids in sight. I'm still looking."

While she raced around the building, she heard the call go out to the volunteer fire department and Chief Gallegos respond that his crews were six minutes out.

"Anybody here?" she called again.

Just faintly, she thought she heard a high cry in response, but her radio crackled with static at that instant and she couldn't be sure. A second later, she heard Cade's voice.

"Bailey, this is Chief Emmett. What's the status of the kids? Over."

She hurried back to her vehicle and popped the trunk. "I can't see them," she answered tersely, digging for a couple of water bottles and an extra T-shirt she kept back there. "I'm going in."

"Negative!" Cade's urgency fairly crackled through the radio. "The first fire crew's ETA is now four minutes. Stand down."

She turned back to the fire and was almost positive the flames seemed to be crackling louder, the smoke billowing higher into the sky. She couldn't stand the thought of children being caught inside that hellish scene. She couldn't. She pushed away the memory of those tiny charred bodies.

Maybe whoever had tripped Darwin's alarms— maybe the same kids who likely set the fire—had run off into the surrounding trees. She hoped so, she really did, but her gut told her otherwise.

In four minutes, they could be burned to a crisp, just like those sweet little kids in Boise. She had to take a look.

It's what her father would have done.

You know what John Wayne would say, John Bailey's voice seemed to echo in her head. *Courage is being scared to death but saddling up anyway.*

Yeah, Dad. I know.

Her hands were sweaty with fear, but she pushed past it and focused on the situation at hand. "I'm going in," she repeated.

"Stand down, Officer Bailey. That is a direct order."

Cade ran a fairly casual—though efficient—police department and rarely pushed rank, but right now he sounded hard, dangerous.

She paused for only a second, her attention caught by sunlight glinting off one of the bikes.

"Wynona, do you copy?" Cade demanded.

She couldn't do it. She couldn't stand out here and wait for the fire department. Time was of the essence, she knew it in her bones. After five years as a police officer, she had learned to rely on her instincts and she couldn't ignore them now.

She was just going to have to disregard his order and deal with his fury later.

"I can't hear you," she lied. "Sorry. You're crackling out."

She squelched her radio to keep him out of her ears, ripped the T-shirt and doused it with her water bottle, then held it to her mouth and pushed inside.

The shift from sunlight to smoke and darkness inside

the barn was disorienting. As she had seen from outside, the flames seemed to be limited for now to the upper hayloft of the barn, but the air was thick and acrid.

"Hello?" she called out. "Anybody here?"

"Yes! Help!"

"Please help!"

Two distinct, high, terrified voices came from the far end of the barn.

"Okay. Okay," she called back, her heart pounding fiercely. "Keep talking so I can follow your voice."

There was a momentary pause. "What should we say?"

"Sing a song. How about 'Jingle Bells'? Here. I'll start."

She started the words off and then stopped when she heard two young voices singing the words between sobs. She whispered a quick prayer for help and courage, then rapidly picked her way over rubble and debris as she followed the song to its source, which turned out to be two white-faced, terrified boys she knew.

Caleb and Lucas Keegan were crouched together just below a ladder up to the loft, where the flames sizzled and popped overhead.

Caleb, the older of the two, was stretched out on the ground, his leg bent at an unnatural angle.

"Hey, Caleb. Hey, Luke."

They both sobbed when they spotted her. "Officer Bailey. We didn't mean to start the fire! We didn't mean to!" Luke, the younger one, was close to hysteria, but she didn't have time to calm him.

"We can worry about that later. Right now, we need to get out of here."

"We tried, but Caleb broked his leg! He fell and he

can't walk. I was trying to pull him out, but I'm not strong enough."

"I told him to go without me," the older boy, no more than ten, said through tears. "I screamed and screamed at him, but he wouldn't go."

"We're all getting out of here." She ripped the wet cloth in half and handed a section to each boy.

Yeah, she knew the whole adage—taught by the airline industry, anyway—about taking care of yourself before turning your attention to helping others, but this case was worth an exception.

"Caleb, I'm going to pick you up. It's going to hurt, especially if I bump that broken leg of yours, but I don't have time to give you first aid."

"It doesn't matter. I don't care. Do what you have to do. We have to get Luke out of here!"

Her eyes burned from the smoke and her throat felt tight and achy. If she had time to spare, she would have wept at the boy's quiet courage. "I'm sorry," she whispered. She scooped him up into a fireman's carry, finally appreciating the efficiency of the hold. He probably weighed close to eighty pounds, but adrenaline gave her strength.

Over the crackles and crashes overhead, she heard him swallow a scream as his ankle bumped against her.

"Luke, grab hold of my belt buckle, right there in the back. That's it. Do not let go, no matter what. You hear me?"

"Yes," the boy whispered.

"I can't carry you both. I wish I could. You ready?"

"I'm scared," Luke whimpered through the wet T-shirt wrapped around his mouth.

So am I, kiddo. She forced a confident smile she

was far from feeling. "Stay close to me. We're tough. We can do this."

The pep talk was meant for herself, more than the boys. Flames had finally begun crawling down the side of the barn and it didn't take long for the fire to slither its way through the old hay and debris scattered through the place.

She did *not* want to run through those flames, but her dad's voice seemed to ring again in her ears.

You never know how strong you are until being strong is the only choice you've got.

Okay, okay. She got it, already.

She ran toward the door, keeping Caleb on her shoulder with one hand while she wrapped her other around Luke's neck.

They were just feet from the door when the younger boy stumbled and went down. She could hear the flames growling louder and knew the dry, rotten barn wood was going to combust any second.

With no time to spare, she half lifted him with her other arm and dragged them all through the door and into the sunshine while the fire licked and growled at their heels.

* * * * *

Don't miss RIVERBEND ROAD by New York Times bestselling author RaeAnne Thayne, available July 2016 wherever HQN books and ebooks are sold.
www.Harlequin.com

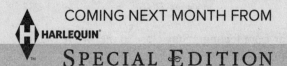

COMING NEXT MONTH FROM

SPECIAL EDITION

Available July 19, 2016

#2491 HER MAVERICK M.D.
Montana Mavericks: The Baby Bonanza • by Teresa Southwick
Nurse Dawn Laramie refuses to fall for a doctor she works with and put her job at risk...*again*! But Jonathon Clifton won't let her cold shoulder get to him. When these two finally bury the hatchet and become friends, will they be able to resist the wild attraction between them?

#2492 AN UNLIKELY DADDY
Conard County: The Next Generation • by Rachel Lee
Pregnant widow Marisa Hayes is still grieving her husband's death when his best friend, Ryker Tremaine, arrives on her doorstep. He promised to watch out for Marisa in case anything happened to Johnny, but the more time he spends with her, the more he longs to help her through her grief to a new life—and love—with him.

#2493 HIS BADGE, HER BABY...THEIR FAMILY?
Men of the West • by Stella Bagwell
Geena and Vince Parcell were married once before, until the stress of Vince's job as a police detective took its toll. Six years later, when Geena shows up in Carson City pregnant and missing her memories, they have a second chance at becoming the family they always wanted.

#2494 A DOG AND A DIAMOND
The McKinnels of Jewell Rock • by Rachael Johns
The closest thing Chelsea Porter has to a family is her beloved dog. When she attends the McKinnel family Thanksgiving with Callum McKinnel, she finds the love and warmth she's always craved. Can they work through their fears from the past to make a future together?

#2495 ALWAYS THE BEST MAN
Crimson, Colorado • by Michelle Major
After a nasty divorce, Emily Whittaker is back in Crimson with her son. Jase Crenshaw thought he was over his high school crush on Emily, but when they team up as best man and maid of honor for her brother's wedding, Jase thinks he's finally found his chance to win the girl of his dreams...

#2496 THE DOCTOR'S RUNAWAY FIANCÉE
Rx for Love • by Cindy Kirk
When Sylvie Thorne broke their engagement, Dr. Andrew O'Shea realized he didn't know the woman he loved at all. So when he finds out she's in Wyoming, he decides to get some answers. Sylvie still thinks she made the right decision, but when Andrew moves in to get closure, she's not sure she'll be able to resist the man he becomes away from his high-society family.

**YOU CAN FIND MORE INFORMATION ON UPCOMING HARLEQUIN® TITLES,
FREE EXCERPTS AND MORE AT WWW.HARLEQUIN.COM.**

HSECNM0716

SPECIAL EXCERPT FROM

 HARLEQUIN®

SPECIAL EDITION

*Can secret agent Ryker Tremaine help his best friend's
pregnant widow, Marisa Hayes, overcome her grief
and make a new life—and love—with him?*

Read on for a sneak preview of
AN UNLIKELY DADDY,
the next book in New York Times *bestselling author
Rachel Lee's long-running miniseries*
CONARD COUNTY: THE NEXT GENERATION.

"Am I awful?"

"Awful? What in the world would make you think that?"

"Because…because…" She put her face in her hands.

At once Ryker squatted beside her, worried, touching her arm. "Marisa? What's wrong?"

"Nothing. It's just… I shouldn't be having these feelings."

"What feelings?" Suicidal thoughts? Urges to kill someone? Fear? The whole palette of emotions lay there waiting for her to choose one.

She kept her face covered. "I have dreams about you."

His entire body leaped. He had dreams about her, too, and not only when he was sleeping. "And?"

"I want you. Is that wrong? I mean…it hasn't been that long…"

Her words deprived him of breath. He could have lifted her right then and carried her to her bed. He'd have done so joyfully. But caution and maybe even some wisdom held him back.

"I want you, too," he said huskily.

She dropped her hands, her wondering eyes meeting his almost shyly. "Really? Looking like this?"

"You're beautiful looking just like that. But…"

"But?" She seized on the word, some of the wonder leaving her face.

"I don't want you to regret it. So how about we spend more time talking to each other? Give yourself some time to be sure. Hell, it probably wouldn't be safe anyway."

"My doc says it would."

She'd asked her doctor? A thousand explosions went off in his head, leaving him almost blind. He cleared his throat. "Uh…I could take you right now. I want to. So, please, don't be embarrassed. I don't think you're awful. But…please… get to know me a bit better. I want to know you better. I want you to be sure."

"I feel guilty," she admitted. "It's been driving me nuts. Am I betraying Johnny?"

"I don't believe he'd think so. But that's a question only you can answer, and you need to do that for yourself. Then there's me."

"You?" She studied him.

"I don't exactly feel right about this. After what you've already been through, I shouldn't have to explain that. I'm just like John, Marisa. Why in the world would you want to risk that again?"

She nodded slowly, looking down at where her fingertips pressed into the wooden table. "I don't know," she finally said quietly.

Don't miss
AN UNLIKELY DADDY
by New York Times *bestselling author Rachel Lee,*
available August 2016 wherever
Harlequin® Special Edition books and ebooks are sold.

www.Harlequin.com